Lau. ....egraph columnist and contributing editor of *She* magazine. The author of several acclaimed novels, the two most recent were *Life According to Lubka* and *At Sea*. She lives in Dublin. Visit her website at www.lauriegraham.com

Praise for Laurie Graham

'It embraces you with warmth and humour and makes the world a better place.'   Katie Fforde

'What a wonderful, life-enhancing, truly funny writer she is.'   Elizabeth Buchan

'Graham wraps serious questions in glorious comedy. This scratchy, snappy heroine, a wonderful mixture of sass and solemnity, is a diverting addition to Graham's collection of highly original adventuresses.'   *Sunday Times*

'She has wit and insight to match Nick Hornby, and the entertainment value of Helen Fielding, as well as depth.'
                                                    Independent

'An exceptional ear for dialogue and a wonderful range of characters.'   *Sunday Express*

'Riveting. ~~Hilarious one-liners fall in quick~~ succession.'
                                                    The Times

'Hugely entertaining clash-of-cultures novel from the razor-sharp Graham ..... a sunny book fo- ...y days.'
                                                    ...aily Mail

Perfect Meringues

Laurie Graham

Quercus

First published in Great Britain in 1997 by Black Swan
This paperback edition published in 2010 by

Quercus
21 Bloomsbury Square
London
WC1A 2NS

A CIP catalogue record for this book is available
from the British Library

ISBN 978 1 84916 470 2

10 9 8 7 6 5 4 3 2 1

Typeset by Ellipsis Books Limited, Glasgow

Printed and bound in Great Britain by Clays Ltd, St Ives plc

This one is for my father

I wrote *Perfect Meringues* in the mid-90's, battling with single parenthood, a fire-breathing bank manager and a publisher's deadline. That I finished it at all was a miracle. Now I look at it and wonder why it seemed such a big deal. But that's because my writing, like my dress size, has expanded with the passing years.

Laurie Graham

I'd been browsing around Surinder Singh's Nip-In in a headscarf, pretending I might buy a frozen dinner, so I could observe the man who might be my next lover and see which Sunday paper he reads. He bought a box of Banana Bubbles and *The Sunday Times*, and then I let him go. The secret of good tailing is knowing when to stop. I bought a bottle of Worcester Sauce to avert suspicion, and then came home. I could hear the smoke alarm before I even had my key in the door.

She hadn't heard it, of course. Hadn't noticed the blue haze either, because she was assembling a triple-decker gut-buster and her Jungle Big Boys CD was playing at full hammer, and also because, inside that big bony head, which I grew and tended like a prize marrow, and evacuated into the world at great cost to my future prospects as a gorgeous piece of snug-fit ass, inside that abnormally large and bony head, the girl has shit for brains.

1

I explained to her, again, what happens if you leave hot bacon fat to get hotter. She sighed.

I said, 'What are you doing?'

'Making a samwidge.'

Bread, bacon, egg, sauce, more bread, more bacon, melted cheese . . . A dripping ziggurat. Her cardigan sleeves are unravelling from the cuffs up, and still they're too long; they reach to her furthest knuckles. Everything she does: drinking tea, applying Clearasil, smoking Low Tars, jacking off gormless Gavin while they're supposed to be revising – it's all done with fingers a quarter of an inch long.

I said, 'But we're having duck.'

Then she told me, with a wad of bread in her mouth, that she was going out. Seeing Alec and his new woman.

'When?'

'Later.'

'Why didn't you say?'

'Forgot.'

'Where are you going?'

'Dunno.'

'When did he phone?'

'Before.'

'Any messages?'

'No.'

She carried her tea bag slowly, drip, drip, drip, to the pedal bin, wondering at my impertinence. *Messages?* For *me?*

I said, 'Eleanor . . .'

And she said, 'God, uh!' and went back to her pit, humphing and drooping with a face like tallow.

I did the duck anyway. Washed it in lavender honey and dried it with the hair-dryer to make the skin go crisp. Just plain roasted, with a salad of watercress and fat black cherries and a cheeky little Merlot from the two pounds ninety-nine end of the vineyard. I caught a soapy whiff from upstairs. She'd decided to play it clean and glowing for Daddy. Lucky Daddy. A shame none of her knickers have made it into the laundry recently. I turned up Sinatra to drown out 'Babylon Shall Fall, Motherfuckers', and wondered whether to do anything else about this man.

A church isn't the easiest place to pull. Especially not a man who looks like he's waiting for someone to pinch his crisps. He is a doll though; I am tempted.

It's stupid even being there really. It's not as though I don't have plenty to do – work; seeing people – but I haven't quite got used to Sundays since Alec went. It used to be our main time together. There weren't so many Sunday shopping opportunities then. You could maybe drive out to a garden centre, buy a pot plant and a bag of toffees, but that was about it. We used to stay in a lot, knee-deep in newspapers, noticing things about each other. *Sucks teeth. Wags foot. Fills cup too full. Breathes in an inconsiderate way.*

We tried not to shout, because of Eleanor. Fourteen waking hours though, most Sundays. Seven hundred hours a year, for ten years. You're bound to miss something like that when it's gone.

I started going to Mass because I liked the feeling that I'd slipped behind enemy lines. In our house we called them 'caddies' and we gave them a wide berth, even Dad's cousin Jimmy Reilly and all that crowd. The Queen was C of E so that was good enough for us. When Jimmy's girls got married we were invited to all the weddings, but Mum always knocked that on the head. She said caddie weddings went on for hours and Dad'd have to keep nipping out. I could have been a bridesmaid several times over if it hadn't been for my dad's bladder and the length of the nuptial Mass.

I like to go to the eleven o'clock. Get there early and watch people arrive. There's a woman with a black thing on her head, like a Spanish widow, and this amazing escaping hair. And there's five men with bad teeth and big red hands, who always come in last and stand at the back. They smoke roll-ups as soon as they get outside. I'd like to meet the joker who sold them a job lot of bright blue suits.

And then there's himself: dark, shy, a bit sad-looking too. The kind of man who maybe had a fiancée, only she married someone else. He fidgets and bumbles, drops his missal, puts his reading glasses on top of his head and then can't find them. And very devout. Does the full

4

floor-grazing dip when he genuflects and strikes his chest at the *mea culpa*. Probably a recent convert.

It was his scarf I noticed first. Lovely soft red wool on one side, yellow paisley lining and a long silky fringe. Quite a style statement for a man who sometimes forgets to tuck his shirt-tail in.

So I followed him, down the road and round the Nip-In, but it's hard to see how I can make a move on a man who mainly looks at the floor.

A girl with clean hair and a flowery dress appeared in my kitchen; I think we may be related. This was in the divorce settlement: I get close daily contact with bad atti-tude and unravelling knitwear, and Alec gets two hours a fortnight with a freshly showered sunbeam. Also, he gets to date girls called Sam, who weren't even born when the Archies had five weeks at Number One with 'Sugar Sugar', and I get to stalk middle-aged men who buy banana-flavoured breakfast products. I guess I should have read the small print.

I said, 'Will you be late?'

'Dunno.'

'What's the plan?'

'Dunno. Tempinbowlin'.'

'Have you finished your Geography?'

'Yeah.'

I knew she hadn't finished her Geography and she knew I knew, but still we go through the motions. I mean, we're not talking oxbow lakes here, or the principal crops of the Murray-Darling basin. We are not talking Geography homework that considers the impact of tree-felling on the habitat of the Guaraní Indian. We are talking colouring in the sea. Eleanor believes Manchester is the cultural capital of the Western world, but she couldn't find it on a map, even if you held a Stanley knife to her throat and told her her life depended on it. 'Up the motorway,' she'd say. No curiosity, no enthusiasm, and just the one facial expression. When she was born the nurse said, 'You have a lovely healthy baby girl,' but I think she's actually some advanced form of fish.

The new woman stayed in the car while Alec and Eleanor re-bonded, but I had a good look. He'd better watch out if he's planning on sitting between the pair of them at the bowling alley. He could get both his eyes put out. *Senior Executive Blinded By Synchronized Hair-Tossers.*

'Oh yeah,' she said, halfway into the car, 'I forgot. Aunty Yvonne phoned. Said go for tea if you like, being as you're all on your own.'

Thank you, Eleanor. I'm not sure if some of the hard of hearing in the outer reaches of Selly Oak with triple-glazed windows actually caught that, but thank you anyway for trying.

I ate too much duck and felt sick. Then I made a Today
list:

    Make lists for week etc.
    Call Yvonne.
    Think what to say to your mother.
    Call Adam and end it.

List for week:
    Dry-cleaning. Light bulbs.
    Gas Consumers' Council.
    Tetanus appointment.
    Apples, quinces? Possibly plums.
    Investigate smell.

List for month:
    VAT.
    Suede shoes.

Get hair cut.

Drink less coffee.

Throw out spices that were best before end 1993.

Rest of Life:

Read proper literature.

Do bum lifts.

Stop saying, 'Yes,' when the operator says, 'Will you hold?'

I called Adam. I said, 'It's only me. I wondered if you fancied dinner some time this week.' Long silence.

'I'm very busy.'

'OK, it was just a thought.'

Even longer silence.

'Was there anything else?'

So I said, 'Look, Adam, this is ridiculous. I mean, we're two grown-up people and we've had some nice evenings over the past year. You know, nice, grown-up, no strings, but the thing is, where is this relationship going, you know? If I don't hear from you in twelve weeks, I mean it's been *twelve* weeks, what am I supposed to . . . you know? Are you trying to say something? I think we need to sit down and talk about . . . us. You know?'

Silence without end.

'This is exactly my point, Adam. I mean if you just sit there not saying anything, how am I supposed to know how you feel about us? That's why I thought dinner . . . How about Tuesday? Or Wednesday?'

'Why don't I call you some time?'

'OK. Have you got someone with you? OK. How's it going?'

'Very well. Very busy.'

'Great. You must be pleased. Family all right? Has your sister recovered from her slipped disc?'

'Yes.'

'Right. Well . . . I'll leave it to you to call me then?'

'Yes.'

'Hope I didn't disturb anything. I thought Sunday, you know, probably as good a time as any. Anyway, mustn't keep you.'

'Goodbye.'

I know, I've ended up giving him another chance. But I'm recording this in my diary, and if he hasn't called me in four weeks time, or six weeks, say, in case he's away at a conference or anything, if he doesn't call in the next six weeks, then it's definitely curtains. The thing with Adam is, you do have to make some allowances because he lives in a world of his own. He gets into that lab and life outside might just as well not exist. I've thrown away so many dinners. He's quite brilliant, of course. Very highly rated in cell-death circles. And he can be lovely, like the time he brought me sugared almonds from Paris. And he's about the right age. He's single. He only wears his nylon over-trousers when the weather's really bad.

Anyway, I've laid my cards on the table. I couldn't have made myself clearer. So it's up to him now. Six weeks. No call and he's history.

Mum phoned. The big question of the day was, should she wait in tomorrow for her window-cleaner? See, he should have come last Monday, because it was the second Monday in the month, only he didn't. Now, should she expect him tomorrow, or not until the next month's second Monday? It's a tough one. Some people might wonder why she'd even think of staying home for a man who's only going to smear a dirty chamois leather across the outside of her windows. She's protecting her reputation. She likes to settle up as soon as a job's done. Doesn't want tradesmen putting it about that she's a bad payer. *Pensioner Bankrupts Small Family Business*.

She said, 'You haven't got much to say for yourself.' It was true. I always feel the news drain out of me the moment I hear her voice. I should have had something ready, some decoy news bulletin for her to squeeze the life out of. It was on my list of things to do, but I don't always do them in the order I write them down.

I told her about Eleanor's school trip to Brontë country. Just threw it to her, like a bone to a dog. 'Me and your father went there,' she said, 'and you should have seen what they were asking for a pot of tea and a scone.' She said Mrs Sanderson keeps inviting her in for cups of coffee, but she's told her she has a sister not well in Coventry and she needs to stay in for the phone. My mother has invented a sister in Coventry so she won't have to go to Mrs Sanderson's for coffee, because once you start hobnobbing with people and getting involved you never know where it'll end. *Coffee Morning Bomb Factory Shock*.

My dad used to claim he'd met Ava Gardner, but only when he'd had more than one Mackeson. So I suppose there is a fanciful tendency in the family, but I don't think I could be bothered inventing a sister. You'd have to think up a name and a whole long history about her. I don't always tell people about Philip, and he's real.

I said, 'What's her name?'

She said, 'Who?'

'This sister. Is she close to death?'

She said, 'There's no call for cleverness.'

I said, 'But no, Mum, think, you can't let her die – ever. You'll have to let her see you out. She's all that stands between you and coffee with Mrs Sanderson. It'll have to be a chronic condition; something that flares up at short notice. And she ought to have a name. Oh what a tangled web we weave . . .'

She said, 'People never used to be in and out of each other's houses. Sometimes you have to tell a little fib, when folks keep angling to get pally.'

I told her about the gas bill I'm querying and about bumping into Megan from college, and then I couldn't think of any more things to tell her about that wouldn't matter if she spoiled them. I just ran at the point of her

11

fruit knife with my breast bared. I said, 'I'm having some new photos done. For the *TV Times*,' and she said, 'Will they send a hairdresser? And some nice tops for you to wear? Your hair has never looked as nice as it did when Auntie Edie permed it.' So there we have it. My mother has despised my hair since 1963.

Alec could work wonders with my mother. To him it was a kind of low-cost light entertainment. He just agreed with everything she said, and then some. It didn't matter how many times he had to contradict himself, he always stayed on the winning team. Always egged her on with lavish noises of encouragement. 'That's right, Muriel, that's right.' She never mentions him now. When I told her we were splitting up she didn't say anything, just plumped the sofa cushions. I'd have quite liked it if she'd called him a bastard, just once, but it's as though Alec never happened. She's like a combine harvester: whatever you chuck in her path she flattens it, and it comes out the other end in a nice compact little parcel that won't be any bother to anyone. If you wanted conflict with my mother you'd have to cut the juice, stop the combine harvester from rolling, only you can't. It's unstoppable.

At home, if anyone produced evidence for the defence, or cross-examined her about her wide-ranging world view, she'd say things, just to keep the air waves busy. 'It wouldn't do if we all thought the same.' That was her 13-amp circuit-breaker. She used that when she thought things were getting too hot. But things never did get too hot. Dad just ate his tea and did as he was told. He'd have jumped off the top of the brickworks chimney if Mum had advised it.

I said, 'We'll come and see you. On a weekend when Eleanor hasn't got too much homework.'

That's what happens. Once she's needled me, I start making rash offers, trying to get her back to a position where she might say something nice. She could have said, '*My* Lizzie. In the *TV Times*! I shall have to tell them all at the Toc H.' But she said, 'There's no need to come specially, I know you're busy. It was on *Woman's Hour* about single-parent families and how the kiddies suffer. And Yvonne and Philip get over once a fortnight.'

Offside again. She's got blood pressure and a hiatus hernia and she needs a nap in the afternoon, and yet she whips round, every time, and leaves me offside.

I did call Yvonne, but not until it was too late to go for tea. She said, 'Don't sit indoors, girl. Come round if you like. There's ham left, and he's out. Kayleigh's in a baton-twirling contest in Lichfield and he's gone along for the ride. Saw you on the telly Thursday. I liked your blouse.'

Philip was born in 1953. I was seven. Nurse Smith came,

14

with a wart between her eyebrows. She said, 'Don't you go bothering your mother.' I never bothered my mother. It was nice after he was born. We got big tins of National dried milk that made great pancakes, and bottles of Welfare orange that I helped Philip to drink. I got new friends too. Susan Carter and Wendy Flitcroft cultivated me after that because they liked babies. He cried a lot, Philip. His top lip and his chin were always sore and his romper elastic dug into his legs. That's what baby boys wore then: smocked rompers, to look like Prince Charles. One time Philip cried because a piece of coal spat out of the fire and startled him, and I got the blame and a red mark from Mum's hand on my leg. It wasn't his fault. Wendy Flitcroft used to come round and bounce him up and down. Then one day he hiccupped on her and she said, 'Your kid smells cheesy.' She stopped coming round, and quite a few people, like about all forty-two members of Top Infants, started calling me Cheesy.

Philip I can take or leave these days. He's very quiet; very slow. If you ask him anything he stays stock still, blinking, and then, just when you've decided he can't have heard you, he answers, but he always sounds like he's trying the answer out, to see if it's the one you wanted.

He's worked at the Leccy Board since he left school, but I'm not sure what he does there. It's something to do with appliances, and sometimes he gets het up about somebody called Brian who doesn't follow correct procedure. That's when his psoriasis comes back, when he's

15

had a run-in with Brian over correct procedure. I do know they have cream cakes all round on people's birthdays.

Yvonne worked for the Board too, in the wages office. She asked Philip out because he was a bit backward at coming forward, and then, later on, she told him they might as well get married. She left wages just before she had Kayleigh and never went back. She did payroll for a few people from home – small businesses. She's very good with figures. The time we all went to the Gardenia for pizzas she just ran her eye down the bill and she knew straight off it was wrong.

After the bookkeeping she did selling: carpet shampoos, venetian-blind brushes, stuff like that – selling to neighbours and anybody she knew. I was glad when she packed that in; the cans of oven cleaner were piling up mightily. Then after Scott was born she did diet counselling for Trim-Tru. And now she's a colour consultant. Fifty quid to play with her fabric swatches for an hour and find out whether you can really wear mauve. I like Yvonne.

Eleanor played up this morning. Said she ached everywhere and she'd only got Social Studies and Information Technology, so shouldn't she stay home and not infect people? I made her go. How can I concentrate on what I'm doing knowing she's on the loose? Boiling empty kettles and dyeing her hair without doing a test strand. Then the traffic was backing up to the Ivy Bush, and I got a less than charming reception from Alison when I did eventually get to the studio. She said, 'We're cutting you by four minutes and moving stars for the week to Tuesday. We've had to make room for some religious miracle in Sparkbrook. So decide what you're going to drop and then get yourself into make-up.' The running order was French Manicures, Surrogate Mothers (with viewers' phone calls), Recipes for that Glut of Apples, the Milk-Drinking Statue – Miracle or Hoax? and Patchwork Quilts for the Nineties.

Stuart was going through his notes with Meredith and

the new production assistant. No sign of Kim. I went into make-up and she wasn't there either. Tiff put the little plastic cape on me and mouthed, 'She's in the la-la. Not very well.' You get the full grimacing works from Tiff when she's divulging things about someone who may just be within a ten-mile radius. Eyes rolling towards the last-known location of, mouth gurning and shuddering away, whether it's good news or bad. Bad is her speciality. Anyway, the salient points were, Kim had turned up in a short skirt and high-gloss tights, Meredith had said her legs looked like pork sausages and she should lay off the Danish pastries, Stuart had pitched in and said it could be water retention – he'd been reading about it in *New Woman* – and he thought she looked great, really great for forty-six, and Kim had run off the set saying she quit and none of it was any of Stuart's fucking business, and anyway, as he perfectly well knew, she was only thirty-eight. *Star Kim In Birth Certificate Mix-Up*.

Tiff said, 'So she's still in there. I'm going to have to do her right from scratch when she comes out. Look up for me, don't blink. And let's face it, even Pan-Stik's got its limits. I'm just going to put some more concealer on your dark circles. You ought to try sleeping with the window open. And the thing is, if she does the show looking blotchy it reflects very badly on me. People write in. Make a nice big mouth for me. Did you do anything at the weekend? We ordered our new settee. They've got an Autumn Price Slash Extravaganza at World of Leather.

Twelve weeks for delivery. Nice big mouth again. And Saturday night we went to a party out in Rubery. Six Malibu and lemonades and I didn't feel as if I'd had a drop. See, I think, with Kim, it's comfort eating. You know? I mean' – pause for scene-setting convulsion of the lips – 'her marriage isn't everything it could be, and when you're going through a bad patch, let's face it, you keep going to the biscuit tin.'

Biscuit tin. Rice pudding tin. Cake tin containing pieces of ancient royal icing. Cold-potato-and-pork-dripping-containing roasting tin. Apparently, with some women, a foundering love life robs them of their appetite.

'There,' she said, 'I'll just run a brush through your hair, and then I'll check you for shine before you're on. Are you doing apple strudel? I love apple strudel.'

I did rap on the door and ask Kim if she was all right. No reason she should confide in me though. We've always kept our distance. That's the way we both like it. That way she can carry on thinking she's the big star, opening supermarkets and swanning in from Shirley in a studio car, and I can carry on thinking she's a lush who got lucky. I fetched her a coffee and two doughnuts and left them outside the door. She didn't *have* to eat them. I hate it when I have to cut something at the last minute. It's always me they do it to. I'd planned a compote of apples and blackberries, piled into a bread-lined bowl and pressed overnight, like summer pudding; tarte tatin; and softened

19

apple slices with maple syrup on little croutes of butter-fried bread. I wanted to mention quinces as well, and chicken stuffed with tart apples, cayenne and cinnamon, and Cheshire cheese crumbled over hot apples and walnuts and served with a plain green salad. But Meredith came up and said, 'For fuck's sake. How many times do we have to go through this? They like crunchy toppings. Fucking quinces? Are you crazy? This is *Midlands This Morning*, not fucking *Masterchef*. Give them apple crumble. Give them a crunchy fucking topping. Alison, has the Hindu arrived yet?'

The Hindu was in the green room with the surrogate mother and the couple she was hatching the egg for. Louie came and leaned on the counter of the kitchen set while we were setting up. They'd canned his piece for another day. Astrologers get treated worse than cooks, and they definitely get treated worse than experts on needlework who just happen to be the producer's sister. He said, 'The new moon joining Pluto in Sagittarius points to exciting personal and professional developments that will come to fruition in the spring. Someone close to you needs patience and understanding. Your most important task now, though, is to give them a crunchy fucking topping. Hello, heart. How's tricks? I hear Kimmykins is snotting in the facilities again.'

It turned out the Hindu hadn't personally seen any statues drinking milk, but they had to go with him because they'd already trailed the story. We'll probably have to have some top Christian on next week, to keep the balance. I wouldn't have minded being a Hindu. An elephant-headed deity was just what we could have done with at St Luke's. I used to have to take Philip to Sunday school, even after I said I was an atheist. Mum said I was to go anyway, just in case. She said it gave her five minutes. I got a prize one year for good attendance and helping with infants, which was mainly taking them to the toilet. They gave me *A Child's Treasury of Parables*. Christine Tunnadine made a holy Joe mouth at me while I was waiting to go up and get it, and Miss Bassett, who paid for the prizes and gave them out, said, 'Well deserved, young lady. Very well deserved.' I can't really say that it was.

Miss Bassett always wore a collar and tie, and she could reverse an artic out of Bassett's Road Haulage gateway with an inch to spare either side. Christine Tunnadine married a builder from Croft who went bust, and Miss Bassett got the MBE eventually, but when she died they found her in the bath and they said she'd been there for days.

We had a Bible story every week at Sunday school, but the only one I liked was the one about the loaves and fishes. I always imagined Jesus going round Galilee with a big tray of bridge rolls, sardine paste on one side, dressed crab on the other. I remember the Philistines too. They were baddies, so God seemed to give them a good drubbing most weeks. Or was it the Pharisees? I think it was both of them. I think they both came in for quite a lot of wrathful smiting.

They got a lot of viewers' calls about surrogate mothers, all anti. The woman on the West Midlands omnibus evidently doesn't agree that a woman's body is her own to hire out as an incubator. I don't know. I can see there might be problems later on. If the couple kept sending you photos and updates. *As you can see, Gemma has really filled out this year. She's making steady progress on the French horn and shows great promise as an impersonator. Enclosed is a tape of her doing Roger Rabbit.*

Anyway, you could tell the parents were annoyed. Didn't think they'd had enough time to put their point of view across properly. They don't seem to realize you've got to keep things moving along on TV; you can't have long bits with people standing around explaining things. Then Kim did one of those tricky links. The slightly clouded face she does for thorny issues of the day erupting into full sunshine for fashion, cookery and beauty tips. I have to hand it to her.

'Now,' she said, 'gardeners tell us there's been a bumper crop of apples this year. I know my lawn is covered with them. So if you're tired of apple pie and are wondering what else you can do with them, stay tuned, because after the break we shall be In the Kitchen with Lizzie Partridge.'

I promised Yvonne I'd look in. I took one of the apple and blackberry puddings and a bottle of Mumm, but Yvonne hurried that away to a place of safety. She never wastes good stuff on family.

Scott was out the back, booting his football against the wall, like it was a horrible job somebody was making him do. *Child Labour Scandal In Barr.* When Philip was his age at least he used to jump about a bit and pretend to be Geoff Hurst.

Chops, mash, peas and gravy. Yvonne asked me to make some tomato water lilies. She seems to think that's the kind of thing I do. Kayleigh had had her ears pierced. I'm not being judgemental. Eleanor got hers done at the Charter Fan? and they'd gone septic before I'd even noticed. Kayleigh's won't go septic; she's dabbing them with surgical spirit every five minutes, whereas Eleanor probably applied horse manure to hers. Kayleigh's was a carefully planned operation, the same as buying her 30AA cup brassiere and getting the right brush-on bronzer for when she sang 'Hey Big Spender' at Pontine. There's something that bothers me about that kid.

Philip wanted meat, potatoes and peas, but no gravy; Kayleigh wanted just meat and gravy; and Scott wanted potatoes and meat with gravy, but all separate and nothing touching anything else. Yvonne had a diet shake.

She said, 'Alec still with the same girl? Eleanor get on all right with her? You seeing anybody yet? What happened to what's-his-face? I can't understand it. You're not bad looking. Got your own house. Nice job on the telly. How about the one who does the news and weather at the weekend? With the beard? Does Birthday Club with the puppy-dog puppet sometimes? He's divorced. It was in my magazine. You want to get yourself fixed up, girl, before your jowls start going. You don't want to leave it too long. Once your jowls have gone it'll be widowers with prostates. You could wear pink, you know. A really strong acid pink.'

Scott was squashing his potatoes with the back of his fork, watching me with his hard little rabbit-dropping eyes. He said, 'D'you know Jet off *Gladiators*? D'you know Wolf? D'you know Mr Motivator?'

I don't know what degree of warmth you're supposed to feel for an only nephew.

I said, 'I'm not looking to get fixed up. I'm happy the way I am. I see Adam. I see Robert.'

She said, 'I thought that was all off. I thought you said he'd got a mother.'

24

I said, 'Not at all. It's just that we're both very busy. I'm seeing him next week, as a matter of fact. Dinner. And we've been talking about a holiday. We might drive down to the Languedoc for a bit of late sun.' If you're going to tell lies, tell them whoppingly big.

She said, 'Well, I'd like to see you fixed up. You make the place look untidy.'

She doesn't look well, Yvonne. She didn't even finish her shake.

So I had to phone Robert. Not *had* to, but his name had cropped up and I thought he might be worth another try. There's nothing else on the horizon. I did see the man from church who wears the nice scarf, but he was in Presto's buying own-brand coffee powder and talking to himself.

Robert wasn't home. His mother said he was out seeing a film. I wonder who with? He could have asked me. The trouble is, everybody thinks I'm out every night at glittering media events, that's why they don't ask me.

I left a message with her, but I know what she'll say when he gets home. 'Some *girl* phoned.' She says *girl* the way most people say 'Nazi'. Or she might not tell him at all. I've got a feeling she picks and chooses which ones to tell him about. Any that sound like they might have covetous designs on her Waterford-type crystal, she probably doesn't write down. Sometimes he doesn't call back and I think that's why. As soon as I'd made that call I wished I hadn't. Robert doesn't want to have dinner with me, and actually I don't want to have dinner with him. He always says, 'I'd best be cutting along. I've got an early start in the morning and Mother's had a few falls recently.' I bet she has. Hurling herself onto the shag pile when she hears his key in the lock.

I made a stack of cinnamon toast, with too much butter, and wrote a list:

Water filters.

Try ginger and lime with chicory.

Birthday card for Philip.

Immac.

Pay phone bill.

Chromium deficiency?

A4 envelopes.

Amaretti.

Eleanor's not at all well, but I think I can be forgiven for not taking her seriously. She'd do anything for an Elastoplast when she was little, and most of the time now she looks like something they dragged out of the canal and zipped into a body bag. I don't see her that much. She's up in her room; I'm down here. And she hates having to eat proper food and sit at a table. She likes it best when I'm off doing a road show or something and she can just nuke herself a pizza. *Home Alone Beriberi Child: TV Cook Charged.* Anyway, her glands are swollen, and I guess even Eleanor couldn't fake that.

She cuddled up next to me. Her hair smelled sour. Mothers aren't supposed to mind things like that. Funny, you never notice exactly when the cuddling stops, or cutting up their food. You never think, 'Right, this is the last time I'm ever wiping *your* bottom.' Ages afterwards, though, you do wonder.

I feel badly about Eleanor. It can't be easy for her, having a strong successful mother to live up to. And she puts on a brave face about Alec, but it must be hard having a deluded old tart for a dad, with a different girlfriend every time you see him. I tried not to hurry the cuddle, and I told her, when she's feeling better, we'll go out for a burger and get her a new pair of jeans. But she trumped that with Alec's latest promise: he's offered to do his spare room up for her, so it's like a little home from home when she goes to stay.

I said, 'But you never go to stay.'

'No,' she said, 'but I shall after the wedding.'

Louie said, 'On the domestic front you are tending to give more than you take, and you find it hard to let go of the past, but astrologically you will soon have bigger fish to fry. Good morning, heart. Fancy a nice big milky one?'

Louie's my best friend in the whole world. We went for breakfast after Tiff had done my eyes and had coffee and bread pudding twice. I asked him if he thought I should have been told first; if Alec shouldn't have told me himself about getting married, instead of leaving Eleanor to let it slip. He said, 'Of course he should. People have no manners these days,' and then he said, 'You're not bothered though, are you? You weren't hoping he'd come back or anything?' I wasn't. But just because I don't want him back doesn't mean it's all right for somebody else to have him and run down the steps of the register office in a nice little suit. I don't think Louie really understands.

I said, 'What am I supposed to do on the actual day? You know? Eleanor'll be going: new dress, clean hair, the works. Am I supposed to leave the country? Or send them a good luck card? I don't know.'

He said, 'You could wait outside and throw rice. Basmati perfumed with coriander might be nice, or a lovely sticky rice pud with a leatherette skin. Don't worry, petal, he'll be having affairs before you can say, *Very sharp pointy knife suitable for sliding between a man's ribs*. Now, listen up, I've heard Kimmykins may be taking a little holiday. A little R and R at Belvedere Grange to sort out her poor tum-tum. It's not official, just a whisper.'

I said, 'If it is true, I bet they'll make Stuart take a break too, to make it look natural. Get another pair of couch pilots in to fly the show for a couple of weeks.'

Louie said, 'Mm, I bet they will. Maybe they'll book Baboon Breath into the Belvedere at the same time – into the Halitosis Unit. We should suggest it. Send an anonymous note upstairs. Have a whip round if need be; I'd

28

give generously. Morning, Stuart. Mercury and Venus in Gemini are fuelling your desire to undertake a journey. You should take up unexpected travel opportunities. Do you think he heard us?'

Alison came looking for me. She said, 'Taking the Fear Out of Fish, right? You're on straight after Yuppy Flu. Then we're following with camcorder tips. Meredith says the little foil parcels are great, but you'll have to scrap the raw cod.'

Louie said, 'See! Fish! What did I tell you? It was in your stars. I'm wasted in this place.' He was on between Best Buys in Hold-Up Stockings and The Dog Who Walked 150 Miles To Get Home. 'Anyway,' he said, 'enough about you, let's talk about me. I'm in love.'

Haddock fillets with tomato and mozzarella was as racy as Meredith was prepared to let things get this morning. He was delirious about the fish pie though. He liked the cheese and potato topping. He said, 'Exactly. *That's* the kind of food we want. That's the kind of food *real* people eat; not raw fucking cod.'

I called Yvonne when I got a minute, to see whether she could take any seviche off my hands. She said, 'I'm glad you phoned. I'm having a lingerie party and you're invited. Tell me again, what is it?'

I told her. 'Just cod with lemons and chilli.'

'But not cooked?'

I said, 'It looks cooked.'

'Well,' she said, 'bung a bit in a dish and drop it off.

I'll give it to Phil. A bit of bread and butter and it'll probably go down. You know Philip; he'll eat it as long as he doesn't see how it's spelt.

Sixteen weeks and five days now since any meaningful contact with Adam; seven weeks exactly since Robert's mother tugged on the umbilical cord and reeled him back in. Alec's dumped Samantha, found Nikki and named the day. Eleanor's seen Gavin for Maths homework and snogging three times a week at least. Tiff must have had about a hundred blissy married moments with her Neil. Even Louie's met someone. He's got tickets for *Idomeneo* and a crying, walking, sleeping, talking, living date. Me, I'm going to my sister-in-law's lingerie party.

At least I shan't be home if Robert phones, or Adam. That'll give them something to think about. Expecting me to be waiting about. And the other thing is, I'll be the celebrity guest. I thought I'd take some copies of the *In the Kitchen* recipe book with me. I'll just have them out in the car, for anyone who wants a signed copy. People love signed books.

I shared the lift with Stuart on the way out. He was

going into town to buy some vital educational toy for the infant king. He must be all of six months old by now. Stuart said, 'We want to get him started on shapes. He's very bright. Everyone says how bright he is. And you should see what he eats: stew, potatoes, mashed banana. He'll probably have some of your fish pie, if Dawn caught the show. We had a bad night with him though, so she might have needed a little nap. It's funny, because he's been sleeping through, but last night, Dawn fed him, and he'd only take the one side. Then he was awake again at one and then again at three . . .'

There was more. It's not the first time Stuart has mistaken me for someone who gives a fuck. I tried not to breathe while we were in a confined space. It could be that he has gum disease. It could be that he was sleeping with his mouth open, and something crawled inside, got trapped and died. Something big.

I made a very slightly late entrance at Yvonne's. I thought that'd help establish a few things, such as what a packed schedule I have, how it'd been touch and go whether I'd make it at all, because in my business you never know what celebrity event you might have to dash to next, and that I wasn't that keen to be there anyway, only I didn't want to disappoint Yvonne. A little reserve always pays dividends, I find.

I timed it badly though. I was a bit too late, so everybody was busy talking. Yvonne didn't even break off to announce me or anything.

Philip had been sent out, like the time Mum sent him and Dad out to the rec in a hurricane while she gave me my first packet of Kotex. Scott hadn't been sent out though; he was hanging about, handling the merchandise and asking for money for a Pot Noodle. Yvonne was smiling too much, working out how she could get shot of him without him kicking up. He said to me, "V you ever met the Chuckle Brothers? I have.'

She gave him some money, but he was back in no time, stinking of beef flavour, pretending he'd lost his Game Boy. Her neighbours were all there: little Maureen, two sisters built like barrels, two Anns, a Karen and a Rita. Too many of them really, squeezed into Yvonne's lounge, holding up the lacy gear against themselves and roaring at how they looked. I did try to join in. I always try, but it always goes wrong. I'm always the wrong side of the glass wall. People did talk to me. I think they might have discussed it before I got there and drawn straws, and then the one who's got to try and talk to me gathers herself up for it. I can see them, working up to it, as if they were getting ready to speak to somebody in a wheel-chair, or Princess Margaret. And it isn't because I've got a plum in my mouth because I haven't. It's because I know things. Of course, they could know things too if they wanted to, only they can't be bothered. Knowing stuff can really queer things for you, socially, but I wouldn't want to change. Not now. You get used to it, like an extra finger. I can't ever remember a time when I wasn't the opposite side of the glass to everybody else. Nearly everybody.

I went to Lansdowne Road County Primary School in 1951. It smelled of wax crayons. I'd already worked out reading from *The Gambols* cartoon strip on the back of my Dad's *Sunday Express*, so I asked Mrs Holyoake if I could have something harder than *Janet and John Book 2*. She told me to be quiet and play in the Wendy house if I'd finished my book, and when I asked my mum what *'un mélange de haute qualité de fruits orientaux'* meant on the side of the sauce bottle, she told me to stop making trouble.

School was where I really started noticing things. I noticed that Mrs Holyoake always went out of school if she wasn't on dinner duty, and when she came back she smelled of cough medicine and she was nice all afternoon, but the next day she never remembered anything good you'd done. So I learned to do good things for Mrs Holyoake in the mornings. I also noticed that Mr Griffiths, who took Top Infants, sometimes didn't go straight home to Mrs Griffiths. Sometimes he helped Miss Timms sort out the rounders equipment in her big cupboard. My mum always said to keep well-in with the higher-ups, but even in Middle Infants I could see it made more sense to have the higher-ups keeping in with me. Apart from Susan Carter and Wendy Flitcroft, my main friends were Janet Coleman, who had fits, and Gilda Lakin. I liked her because she looked foreign and no one else at Lansdowne Road was called Gilda, or probably even in the whole world. Sometimes I chose new names for myself. When I was being Madeleine Michelle de St Xupery, I wrote it in the front of all my Enid Blytons.

My biggest enemy in the world was Gillian Glover.

She had a gang and they used to nobble us and thieve our Spangles. They just used brute force though. If they saw us coming out of the sweet shop they'd have us, but they never planned anything. With Gilda and Janet I was in charge. We weren't a gang, but we did need leadership. Janet and Gilda weren't ideas people; the only things they ever suggested were skipping and swapping dolls' clothes. But they liked doing other things, and all the best things we did, like spying on people and building dens and writing letters in code, those were all my ideas.

So there I was, wrong side of the glass as usual, at Yvonne's Silks 'n' Satins Home Shopping evening, laughing too loud at the knickers and Rita's running commentary. I ordered a set of Teen Temptations for Eleanor. Kayleigh said, 'I'm getting them. I'm getting pink and purple and I'm getting pale green. And I'm getting a Pierre Cardin gold-plated charm bracelet, nine pounds ninety-nine from Argos. Are you my mum's sister or my dad's?'

Yvonne brought round a big plate of warmed-up sausage rolls and everybody said they were starting a diet tomorrow. Yvonne doesn't need to; it's dropping off her. I thought someone might say something when she brought the food in. Like, 'Oh, Yvonne, these had better be good, you've got the expert here tonight.' Something like that. But nobody did, and I was glad in the end. It would have been hard to behave like a TV celebrity sitting on a breakfast bar stool in Lynwood Drive.

In the end Scott broke the sausage-roll plate, kicking his legs around after he'd been told to go to his room and watch videos. Yvonne said, 'Right, that's it, I'm going to count to five.' But he was still there when I left, lying in everyone's way with his Power Ranger sound-effect gloves going *swoosh*, and Yvonne must have had time to count to a thousand at least.

I gave in. I'd had Tiff drawing me diagrams of what happens to your skin after fifty and the cashier in Top Shop ignoring me and Yvonne sending me marriage-bureau adverts clipped out of her magazine, so when she phoned, and yet again it was my sister-in-law to tell me the doctor had changed Mum's blood-pressure tablets, and not a man begging me to go lambada dancing, I caved in. I said, 'All right, I'll give it a try, but pretend it's for you. Give the bureau your name. Discretion is vital.' When you're in the public eye you have to be so careful. One word in the wrong quarter and you're all over the tabloids.

She said, 'Discretion be jiggered. That place is top of the range, Lizzie. It's executive. If a man's stumped up that kind of money, he's hardly going to be sitting at home of a morning watching you make fish pie, now, is he? Anyway, they're not going to realize. You're not exactly a household name, are you? I mean, you're not exactly Delia

38

Smith, are you?' Yvonne may be very good with numbers, but she's very naïve about show business.

Eleanor was in an egg because she wants a new personal stereo, but Daddy's wallet has clanged shut. He'll be diverting funds to irrigate the seedling romance, I suppose. Long-stemmed roses. Surprise trips to Venice. I said to her, 'You'd better get used to it. And if this new girl starts wanting babies you're going to have to get in line for Daddy's money.' I figured she might as well have some really annoying prospect to grouse about while she's oxycuting that extra nose she's growing.

I said, 'I'm going out. Back late.'

I bet she was on the phone to Childline before I was at the end of the road. *Personal CD Player Deprivation: The New Teen Tragedy.*

Louie had asked me to have dinner and meet his new man. He said, 'You don't frighten me, you famous TV cook, you. I'm doing chicken with Moroccan salted lemons and you can bring the pud.' So I made a *mille-feuille* of plums and pears, warmed it through in his oven, dusted it with icing sugar and served it with very cold Jersey cream.

He said, 'Smells divine. Will you marry me? No, but tell me what you think of Marc. Tell me in a whisper while I bang a few pans around. Did you notice the shoulders? He's Sagittarius with his moon in Leo, and a nice little garden flat in Sutton.'

I fibbed, and told him they make a lovely couple. Just

because a man ends his name with a 'c', it's no reason for me to take against him. It could be the real thing. Vain though. Admiring his own reflection in the window until Louie closed the blind. And not listening; not really with us; playing with his signet ring. He smiled, but then people with dimples always do. They may be smiling at what you said or they may just be accentuating a winning feature. Actually, Marc made me feel about as welcome as a mouthful of gumboils. He won't last. He'll be off and Louie'll come in a bit subdued one morning, and then it'll all come out. Louie doesn't believe in rushing straight into a new relationship after a setback, though. He always grieves for at least a weekend.

I don't know why he doesn't try me. OK, he's preferred men *so far*, but maybe if he tried a woman, a really nice woman like me, he'd change his mind. You hear of it happening the other way. Somebody Alec worked with had two kids and a wife who'd been a finalist in Miss United Kingdom, and he ran off with the man who used to come in and do the office plants. And Louie does love me. Sometimes he just doesn't see what's staring him in the face.

I had a whisky before I phoned my mother. Then the line was busy so I had another, straight, to prevent the tell-tale clink of ice-cubes.

She didn't want to talk about her blood pressure. I don't think she's got blood pressure. I think it's something got up by the doctor to stop her going on about her bowels. She's in a permanent state of discontent with her bowels. She wants to go every day, because she read somewhere that bits of putrefying meat can hang about inside you for years if you're not careful, and because everybody else seems to go oftener than she does. She knows this because she asks them. When she was here last Boxing Day she asked Eleanor. She said, 'You wouldn't have pimples if you went every day. You haven't been today, I'll bet. Have you? You should go first thing.' And she called through the door to me. She said, 'Are you going to be a long time in there? Are you doing something serious? Because if you are, I'll go to the downstairs one, then you won't have to hurry.' And that's not the worst of it. The worst of it is, I answered her.

So that's what I think the blood pressure thing is. Something her doctor's dreamed up to get her mind off her bowels and stop her asking how often he goes. Anyway, she didn't even want to talk about bowels yesterday; not directly. She wanted to tell me that Mrs Sanderson had stepped in a dog mistake on her way to the RSPB coffee-morning and trampled it all over Mrs Curtis's lounge carpet, which is a pretty thorough vindication of her own refusal to mix with folk. *Pooch Poop Horror For Charity Worker: Bird Woman Hits Out* She also wanted to tell me she'd seen the show. She hadn't intended to, but the other channel was like watching a blizzard because the wind had moved her aerial, so she'd had to make do. Perfect Meringues, Devil Worship in the West Midlands, House-Plant Clinic and three Queen for a Day viewer make-overs, but the thing that had really struck my mother was, why didn't I wear an apron?

'Whisking eggs,' she said, 'and that was quite a nice little blouse you were wearing. Ask them for an apron.'

I said, 'What's the doctor say about your blood pressure?'

She said, 'I'll live, if I'm careful. I could get you an apron from the Betterware man next time he's round.'

I don't know what Yvonne was thinking of; she's done this agency thing in my name, given them my number and everything. A woman phoned: Tonya from Crème de la Crème – Introductions for the Discerning.

She said, 'We have clients drawn from the highest social echelons, business, professionals, personalities, and we guarantee absolute discretion and introductions of the very best quality. We're mailing you our information pack today, with details of our special offer of twenty-five per cent off the price of a six-month membership for applications received before the first of October. When you've completed our questionnaire, why not pop along to our offices for a chat, and see for yourself our unique service for unattached professionals?'

Made a list:
    Strangle Yvonne.
    Crystallized mandarins.
    Watch *All That Jazz*.
    Clear leaves out of gutter.
    Rabbit?
    Hand cream.
    Ask Wilmot's to check tyres.

Meredith said, 'Mm, parkin. You know there must be viewers out there who've never known the smell of home baking. Can we call it something like Granny's parkin? Make it sound even homier. Is it too late to change the fact sheet? What else have we got?' I gave him a slice of the fruit loaf made with dried fruit soaked in cold tea. 'Orgasmic,' he said, 'Oh! Oh! This is fabulous. This is English cooking at its best. Gorgeous. I'm not sure about the banana bread, though: sounds a bit sandals and joss-sticks to me. Is it healthy? Is it Californian? I tell you something I've not had in years: an Eccles cake. I suppose they've died out.'

Louie's hand snaked round him and took a slice of fruit loaf. He said, 'Of course they haven't died out. You're just not looking in the right places. Swanning off to all those sun-dried-tomato lunches in your limo. Driving fast past those little back-street cake shops, splashing the peasants with mud. I'm very partial to a toasted muffin myself.'

Kim was in make-up when I went through, talking eye-bag reductions with Tiff, and in the mood to be friends.

She said, 'I was saying, it should be tax-deductible in our business. A legitimate professional expense. I wouldn't mind a chin tuck as well if my accountant could wangle it. Your face is your fortune. Well, in this lark it is. Lynette Hardiman, do you remember her? Used to anchor for *Look West*. I've known her for years; we were at Radio Wessex together, started there the same week actually. Well, she went west at *Look West*. They said it was over money, and she said she wanted to spend more time with her family, but the real reason was, and I got this from a *very* reliable source, she'd developed turkey neck. Good at her job though – shit hot. But they still got rid of her, and if it could happen to her it could happen to any of us.'

Tiff said, 'I'd be worried about something going wrong. Not that my Neil would even let me, because he wouldn't. But it was in my magazine, about facelifts coming out too tight, and there was this woman who'd had lipo done on her thighs and it was all over the place: dents in one bit and big knotty bulges over the other side. I mean.'

Kim said, 'It wouldn't worry me. You go to the very best. Go to the top man.'

Tiff said, 'This woman had spent thousands. How about a nice soft pink lipstick today? For a change.'

Alison looked in and said, 'Change of running order everyone. The handbell ringers are snarled up in Dudley, so we're going with Decorative Paint Finishes and putting them on at the end. And Kim, the Cancer Awareness Week woman's in the green room, I told her you'd be in for a word.'

Kim looked good; overdone, but you have to, otherwise the cameras make you look like you've been in bed with the flu. Credit where it's due, Tiff's a genius with her little pots and brushes. She said, 'I'm trying taupe along your sockets today. Do you really think she'll have her face done? She'd be off for weeks.' Her voice dropped to a whisper and then cut out completely. Only her lips were moving, but I could still follow her because she was right in close, blending away like the clappers.

She said, 'We heard, well, my Neil heard because he knows her driver, and he reckons Bob's left her. He says his car always used to be outside when he picked Kim up in the morning and there's been no sign of it for weeks. She told him Bob's in Saudi on business, but one of the girls on phone-ins, that one with red hair and a wedge cut, she's heard he's in Redditch with a stewardess from British Midlands. I've smudged you; keep still while I tidy it up. Anyway, I think she's looking better than she was, don't you? Perkier. And I mean, there's a lot of women her age wouldn't think even of *trying* stirrup pants. Let me check your teeth for lipstick.'

Meredith said, 'Smashing show, everybody. Many thanks,' and I heard Tiff asking the cancer lady to take a look at a mole. Louie said, 'As Jupiter meets Pluto on the third you should experience abundant energy and a boost to your bank balance. Any banana bread going begging?'

That was when I noticed the bruise on his temple. 'Just a little farewell gift from Marc,' he said. 'Tiff said she'd covered it. I'll have that parkin as well, if Meredith's not put his name on it, and then let's go and get ratted.'

I said, 'I can't, I've got to drive. I'm taking Eleanor to find out about contact lenses.'

He said, 'All right. You be the grown-up. Come and have a nice white wine and soda and watch me get ratted.'

We went to the place that used to be the Six Bells, but now it's the Devereux with lasagne on the blackboard. Louie had two Jack Daniels at the bar and said, 'Oh pooh.'

I said, 'I knew it wouldn't last.' And he said, 'Well, that *does* make me feel better. You're supposed to say

47

you're shocked and "what a lovely couple, who'd have thought it".'

There was no comforting him. He wanted to suffer.

I said, 'Every time this happens to you, Louie, I just wonder if maybe you're barking up the wrong tree. Maybe you're not so much a queer as an undecided?'

'Oh, no,' he said, 'I'm a definitely decided. And he did have lovely shoulders, you must admit. It's just my insurance; there were one or two pieces not really covered.'

Marc had cleaned him out. Silver mainly: little boxes, paper knives, and a lovely Georgian sugar caster. Cash too; he'd taken all his cash.

He said, 'The worst thing is, he took that silver photo frame with my mother's picture. I expect she's screwed up in a council bin somewhere. She wouldn't like that.'

I thought of going out, after I'd seen him home, and getting him another silver frame, but then he said, 'I don't think I've got another picture of her. She burned everything when she went peculiar. She thought Edgar Hoover was paying the Courtenay Nursing Home to spy on her, and everything went up in smoke. Oh well,' he said, 'fuckadoodledoo. What's the latest on Kimmykins? Here's what I think: Bob's left her for a younger woman and she can't decide whether she's bothered. Next thing, she'll be having a new lease of life and they'll be profiling her in the *Mail on Sunday*. I've seen it all before. She'll probably bring out an exercise video or write a novel or something. I hope she does; I love a bit of triumph over tragedy.

Anyway, what do you mean, *every* time this happens to you? It doesn't happen that much. I do all right. Chas'd have me back tomorrow, like a shot. I'd like to get into videos, you know: *The Stars and Your Career, The Stars and Your Love Life, Pet Star Signs* – that'd be a winner. I've been talking to my agent about it, it's definitely the way to go. You could too. And books, why aren't you doing books?'

I said, 'I did the *Midlands This Morning Cookbook*. That did very well.'

He said, 'No, but proper books that you don't have to send off for with a stamped addressed envelope, and videos – that's the way to go. We've got to get in there. There are millions of morons out there dying to part with their money and we're earning peanuts.'

Four more Jack Daniels before I got him into the car to go home. He said, 'You know your trouble? You hang back too much. You're always hanging back, letting everybody else make fools of themselves. Head prefect, that's you. Head prefect and she's done all her homework. Little Miss Perfect Prefect. You oughta be more spontaneous. Get it wrong sometimes: serve champagne in a burgundy glass, eat cheese from a squeezy tube.'

He noticed I didn't like that.

He said, 'Don't look hurt, you know I love you. But you need to loosen up, heart. You can be ordinary, you don't always have to know stuff. You shouldn't always wait to see what somebody else is doing before you decide your move. I've got an empty glass again. And if you can learn to rub along with the riff-raff, see things from their point of view, give them crunchy toppings, then they'll like you more and you'll become rich and famous, and W. H. Smith's'll have your books in the front of their window, and you'll say, "Louie, thank you for talking tough. Sometimes you have to be cruel to be kind, and thank God you were." Anyway, I can't sit here all afternoon giving you advice, I've got to go home and wash that man right out of my hair. See you, Miss Pluperfect. See you, heart.'

His intentions were good, and he had had six doubles. I mean, he's got a bruised face and all his silver stolen and *he's* giving *me* advice on how to change *my* life. I felt like I'd gone a few rounds with Mike Tyson though. When I got home I made four slices of French toast and ate them fast, leaning over the sink. Then I wrote some lists, and that always puts me in a can-do kind of mood.

Major Goals:
  Make money.
  Look French.
  Be a better mixer.
  Find man.
  Stop bolting food.

Immediate action:
  Call Hegarty.

Give Robert final chance.

Shorten skirts.

Practise friendly expressions in mirror.

Tomorrow:

Move settee.

Nurofen.

Prunes in bacon?

Recipe for Old-Fashioned.

Check Louie's OK.

Hegarty's been my agent for five years now, and the big time is apparently just around the corner. I don't know quite where I feature in his star-studded firmament, but I guess it'd be true to say that when he wakes up in the morning, I'm not the first thing on his mind. He handles people like Ian Dunkerley, Olympic silver and now much in demand for opening sports centres; and Kathy Mansour, the road-sweeper's daughter from Wolverhampton who divorced a rich Kuwaiti and wants to write a novel about her amazing and exciting life. I suppose you could say Hegarty's speciality is fleeting celebrity. He makes a living. These days you only need to be famous once, and after that you can be famous for being famous. And I suppose the biggest gun in Hegarty's arsenal right now is Sandie Mulholland, who's been in the news three times: for having a hit single in 1977; for selling her 'How I Kicked the Booze' story to one of the Sundays; and then for opening a Wild West restaurant that everyone said was doomed to fail and now it's booked solid so you can't get a table on a Saturday until after Christmas. They do stuff like cow-heel soup and black-eyed peas, and it's very popular with the foodie vanguard because it's saved them trekking miles in search of novelty. It's saved them wondering what kind of style statement to make once celeriac's had its day.

She's reckoned to be a bit of a card, Sandie. Ties her hair up in a big African cloth and laughs like a drain. Anyway, Hegarty managed to get her on *Masterchef* as a celebrity judge. To hear him you'd have thought Joanna Lumley had signed with him. I don't know what else he's pulled off recently. It's been a while since we talked.

He said, 'I was just going to call you, doll.'

I said, 'Good news, I hope.'

'Nothing in partic,' he said, 'just thought I'd touch base with you. Don't want you thinking I've forgotten you.'

I told him that was precisely what I was thinking.

He said, 'Is there a problem? Talk to me.' So I told him I thought I should be doing books and videos and all that business Louie had got me fired up about; and I went on about it for an inadvisably long time, without letting Hegarty interrupt with any comforting little telephone noises. He was probably picking Sandie Mulholland's chilli goat hash from between his teeth.

When I stopped he said, 'See what I can do, doll. Books,

videos. Could be a tough nut to crack, I mean I have talked to people.'

I said, 'Who?' and you know, I would have felt a lot happier if he'd had a name to give me. Even one pathetic little made-up name would have been better than 'People.'

I said, 'Hegarty, I'm starting to wonder if you're the best thing for my career,' and he said, 'It's your call, doll. If you ever feel it's time to move on, I'm not going to stand in your way. But you know what it's like in this business: right time, right place. One minute there's nothing much doing, then, kerboom, and Clive Anderson's begging you to do his show. Leave this book thing with me for a day or two. Today's not good, I've got a VAT inspector going through the books and Jen's off with the flu. Let me put out some feelers. Great shows by the way; I hear the shows are great.'

It wasn't supposed to turn out like this. Once you've made it onto TV, you're supposed to be unstoppable. Today *Midlands This Morning*, tomorrow guest appearances on *The Generation Game*; not stalled with a bunch of nobodies, doing the kind of TV people watch till it's time to cash their next giro. Casting my wontons before swine. Shit though, I've done a whole lot better than some of them thought I would.

When I was fifteen they said I should stay on at school. They said I had what it took to go to teacher training college, which was lavish praise at Peakirk Secondary Modern and could have gone to a girl's head. But at that time I liked the idea of a job with a good-looking uniform, such as BOAC cabin crew, or being a brilliant criminal lawyer in black stockings and those crisply starched bands, and the careers department, which was a box of pamphlets on Whiskery Warrington's desk, didn't have any information on either of those. I knew I'd do something, though. Leave them gasping. When I fell out with Janet Coleman, she said, 'Yeah. Lah-di-dah Clarke. Swanky Clarke. You're going to marry somebody like Rodney Pooley and get a hostess trolley and After Eight mints.' I guess it was the cruellest jibe she could think of, but she was well wide of the mark. Especially the bit about Rodney Pooley and the hostess trolley.

Nobody in our family had ever been to college. Nor

prison. Nor America. Years later I met this D.Phil from Oxford who kept missing *Northern Exposure* because she couldn't work out how to programme her VCR, and I thought Jeez, Oxford; I could have set that place alight. I could have worn Biba dresses and studied Oriental Languages or Nuclear Physics and been president of the Union and everything. But my mum said if I went away to college it'd kill my dad, which, looking back, I doubt, because the Japs hadn't managed it. So on that upbeat note I got a job at Halford's Car Parts and Accessories, selling little rubber floor mats and steering-wheel covers in a stylish choice of ocelot, Black Watch tartan, or leatherette.

I was the only girl. There were two part-timers who used to leave in time to get their kids from school, but they stuck together, consulting each other about pressure cookers and tricky bits in their knitting patterns. I was the real female interest. And the kind of interest I aroused in the Halford's blokes was, if a customer came in and asked for a nipple for a grease gun, they'd go red and look across to see if I'd heard the 'N' word.

I was there two years and I shone like a star. I cleaned up the staff rest-room and bought a sugar bowl out of petty cash to discourage them from spooning it straight from the bag, and I improved the soap situation in the toilet. But I'd gone about as far as I could at Halford's and I still didn't know which way I should be heading next.

There was a bookshop I used to go to in my lunch-hour sometimes, when the smell of nylon overalls and the talk of camshafts got too much; just to look, not to buy. My money was all spoken for, portioned out: board for my mum, shoes, clothes and savings. I was saving up to get away, so when I knew where I wanted to go, I could be off. I kept a little bag ready too, packed with my most important things. I gradually revised what were my most important things and the signed photos of Roy Orbison got the heave ho. I never did go anywhere, not in the dead of night with one small bag at any rate, but I liked knowing it was there, that bag in the wardrobe and the money in the Post Office, ready for an emergency exit.

Anyway, I used to go to the bookshop because it was warm and no one bothered you and they had interesting things. And I found this little book one day, half a crown and still in its dust-jacket. *An Arabian Kitchen*. I tell you. Pistachios and honey and rosewater, vine leaves and walnuts and mint and garlic, and a kind of pastry, the book said, that was thin as paper. I'd just had my packed lunch – mousetrap on white sliced with margarine. That was when I knew what I wanted to do.

I enrolled at the Tech for Catering Level One and got a weekend job waitressing wedding receptions and bar mitzvahs at the Evington Lodge Hotel. Mum said she supposed it'd mean more expense. I don't know what she meant by *more* expense. Our Philip was the one knocking the guts out of his school shoes every five minutes. Halford's were sorry to see me go; they presented me with a road atlas of the British Isles, for when I got a car, and I read it, cover to cover.

The Tech was a bit of a let-down. I wanted to cook things that made people smile and come back for more. I'd started dreaming about food, in full-colour smell-ovision. Lemons, hot bread, onions fried till they were the colour of toffee. But I had to write an essay on sources of food poisoning, and the coley we cooked came in frozen 50lb blocks. I jacked it in when we got to the role of butter-pat machines in portion control, and I went as a strudel trainee to Dauber's Continental Bakery. Between batches I used to come through in my whites and help out front if it got busy. I expect Environmental Health'd do you for that now. Anyway, that's how I met Alec, with flour on my nose, and that's how I met Mrs Fox and started doing dinner parties for her once a month, which is where I met Tom Smith from the *Mercury* and did a few recipes for him whenever he'd got space to fill on the women's page, and finished up doing it daily, and weekly on Radio Leicester too. Pancake advice on Shrove Tuesday, stuff like that.

Hegarty came into my life after I'd done a couple of things for *Good Housekeeping* and somebody said I should get an agent and they knew the very man. I was Mrs Alec Partridge by then and we did sometimes serve after-dinner mints. We also knew we'd made a very big mistake.

Eleanor was home from seeing Alec and his woman earlier than I'd expected. She just glowered past us and thumped upstairs, with her backside hanging out of her distressed jeans. We'd had pork chops, fried with shallots and thyme and simmered in sherry vinegar, garlicky potatoes, green salad, and an ice-cold lemon soufflé, and it had been a bit of a triumph getting him to come to the house at all, but, to tell the truth, I knew I'd reached the end of the line with Robert.

It always had to be somewhere *out* with him, because he's got his mother and my place might be booby-trapped with powerful female hormones. Always a film or a pizza, and I don't even like pizza any more. I lie awake half the night feeling like I've swallowed an army blanket. I suppose it's saved us both having to go through the stuff you do when you go to someone's house. *Feign interest in kitchen extension. Make ostentatious use of coaster mats. Take three goes to flush lavatory. Notice* Lord of the

Rings *on bookshelf*. And he did make it clear from the start that he wasn't ready for 'Anything Serious'. Coming here for dinner really worried him. If you've never lived with a teenager you probably imagine all kinds of terrible things, like she might start having an eating disorder, right within earshot, or turn out to be gorgeously dewy and obviously attracted to the older man, putting you in a very difficult position *vis-à-vis* her desiccated old mother. I think Robert expected embarrassing girlie items to be lying around, and now it's over, now I can't believe I wasted so much time on a man who lets his mother change his sheets, I wish I'd had more fun out of him. I could have had little onyx dishes of tampons on the coffee-table.

I went up to Eleanor after he'd gone. Alec has apparently had a change of mind, brought on, no doubt, by the hair-tossing teen-bride clamping her hand round his balls. It's still to be a Christmas wedding, but in St Lucia, followed by an island-hopping honeymoon and a permanent move to Boston, Massachusetts, in the spring. This had put a crimp in Eleanor's day, not to say an iceberg-sized hole in her hopes for new wedding clothes and fun-packed weekends with a generous young stepmother. Also, though I don't suppose Eleanor's brain has shuffled this far yet, if Alec really goes to town on this wedding in paradise, she'll be lucky to get a Boots voucher for Christmas.

I'm glad he's going. Now perhaps she'll realize he's full of big talk.

Alec phoned later. He said, 'We've been talking. Nikki thinks Elly was upset about the wedding, so what we thought was, she could come with us, be a witness or a bridesmaid or something, and then fly home after the wedding. She'd be back in time for school. It might mess up your plans for Christmas though. Or maybe it won't? I hear you're dating.'

A no-comment situation, I decided.

I said, 'This'd better not be more of your idle chat, Alec. I don't want you saying a word to her till it's definite. And what about Boston? When's she ever going to see you?'

He said, 'It is definite, and Boston needn't be a problem. She'll be able to visit, but I mean . . . this is a company move you know; this isn't some idle whim. I mean, for Chrissakes, and I've gotta give Nikki a chance. You know. I mean, they get on great, but we're entitled to a bit of life, entitled to a bit of time. She knows she'll be coming to visit us; it just won't be so often. Let me talk to her. Put her on. Let me tell her about St Lucia. Has she got a passport?'

So, home alone. Five weeks to find myself a date for Christmas, or fake going to Wiltshire to stay with mystery friends. I could do that. Keep the curtains closed, let the machine answer the phone, have a baked potato with grated cheese and watch my Woody Allen videos.

Yvonne said, 'What friends in Wiltshire? I've never heard you mention any friends in Wiltshire. You can come to us; your mum's coming and one extra's nothing. Did that agency ring you? Little Maureen says her sister tried them and they've got hundreds of men.'

Great. I wonder if she's alerted Reuters about it. I'm going to be a public laughing-stock.

That Tonya was a piece of work; so thin you could see the whites of her knee caps, and everything pulled as tight as a drum, everything except the skin on the back of her hands, that's always the giveaway. Mid-fifties, I'd say, with a big sparkly eternity ring and a voice like sugar underfoot.

She said, 'Here at Crème de la Crème we offer a very special service, my dear. This isn't computer dating. We match people very carefully from our confidential executive register, and our results speak for themselves. We've had weddings. We get engagements. We offer a first-class service for first-class people and we make a difference in people's lives. On our books we have many professional gentlemen who simply haven't had time to find a partner. People lead such hectic lives these days. I'm sure you do. I've been blessed with a good man for thirty-one years myself, but if I had to start looking for someone now, I wouldn't have the time. Busy, busy, busy. And there just isn't the time to go to the tennis club and meet people. Now the other thing about us, my dear, is that we are for the discerning client. Our gentlemen are looking for partners they can feel confident about, ladies they can take out wining and dining and be sure she's not going to use the wrong fork. And I know I can say that to you and you'll understand exactly what I mean.'

Bride Jilted After Cutlery Gaffe.

I said, 'So you turn some people away?' Let it be me. Let it be me.

She said, 'It happens. You see I don't believe in giving people false expectations, and quite honestly, if a lady comes to me and she's not got the savoir fairy or, say, she needs to trim down, I tell her. It isn't easy, but I know she'll thank me in the long run. I say to her, "I'm a professional, so let's be professional about this. This is a very competitive business. My books are full of size tens with letters after their names." Sometimes it's not a matter of turning them down; they just need guidance, and we can give it. We can point them in the right direction and when they come back looking fabulous, knowing how to carry on at select venues with select people, then we can really talk.'

I was beginning to regret a few things: the brown bag with the navy shoes; the half-litre of Belgian chocolate ice-cream I ate last night; being born.

The girl from the outside office came in with coffee

and said, 'What a lovely scarf.' That's her routine, learned from Tonya. Waft freshly brewed hospitality under your nose, offer you a dainty compliment and then retire, so the maestro can go in for the kill.

Tonya said, 'Tell me, my dear, are you between hairdressers?'

Somehow my mother and this woman have made contact and worked together to design my humiliation. She said, 'Because my opinion is, none of us ladies needs to put up with grey these days, you know? Even if it's just a little wash-in wash-out rinse from Boots. Or I can put you on to my man; there's no one to touch him for cutting, and he's got a very good colourist works for him as well; a little black girl but very good. And another important point is, general grooming. Gentlemen hate slovenliness in a lady. Now I know what it's like, you've got a thousand and one things to do, so you dab on your lipstick as you're running out the door and hope for the best. We've all done it, but you know, it's a false economy. We owe it to ourselves to find time for that manicure and that leg wax. And let me give you another little tip: organization. Rearrange your wardrobe so all your blue jackets are together, all your reds, and so on. And the same with your shoes and bags and your little scarves. Everything bandbox fresh and hung up ready to go, so you can see at a glance and choose your outfit. It saves all that worry. Saves you just grabbing the first thing you see and feeling less than fabulous all day long. Hm? Now, let's have a look at your questionnaire. I see you mention belly-dancing. Was that something you saw on holiday? We saw some in Turkey, and they got people up out of the audience to join in.'

I told her it was a genuine hobby, performed barefoot in my own kitchen to 'Rhythms of the Nile' and *Um Kalthoum's Greatest Hits*. I even offered to give her a demonstration, but she said, 'Well, if you'll be guided by me on this one, I suggest we don't mention it straight off. It's one of those things, I mean, I'm sure it can be a lovely thing when it's done artistically, but it's one of those things that could give . . . an impression. Is there something else we could put down instead? I see you've got Gershwin; we'll call that songs from the shows. That's always a good one. How about golf? Or bridge? Or sailing? That's a popular one with some of our gentlemen. We get a lot of them looking for a nice sporty lady to crew for them.'

I could have told her I like eating mango in the bath, and popping the blisters on bubble-wrap, but I don't think she'd have written them down.

I'd been with her an hour and a half and I hadn't even seen any photos. For all I knew her register could have been full of old gits in cravats looking for someone to carry their clubs round eighteen holes every Sunday. 'Sand wedge, Lizzie. Look sharp.'

I said, 'Wouldn't it be easier if I just looked through your albums and picked out the ones I like the look of?'

She said, 'This isn't a livestock market. We match people by their interests and aspirations, and I would suggest that we put in some more work on your personal profile. It's your shop window, so I'm going to ask you to think hard about first impressions. Outrageous doesn't sell. Show-off brainy doesn't sell. Wacko definitely doesn't sell. Keep it simple, keep it nice, keep it badminton and Andrew Lloyd Webber. Do you see what I mean? And the other advice I'd give you is, a couple of weeks on the Hip and Thigh Diet, and an appointment with my Mr Antony. I'll give you his number; tell him I sent you, if you like. I promise you, when it comes to dull lifeless hair, there's nobody to touch him.'

Yvonne said, 'Diet shakes, they're the thing. Saves all that messing around with salads. I've got a cupboard full if you want to start tonight. Course, your trouble is you have to spend too much time thinking about food. I don't. If I don't feel like cooking they just do themselves something in the microwave. Done, eaten, plate in the dishwasher, finished. But it can't be so easy if you've got apple crumbles and things sitting on the side.'

I hadn't seen her for a week or two. She looks terrible. Philip was there, putting a plug on the iron. When she'd gone to find a carrier bag for me, I said, 'She's losing too much weight. Do you realize how skinny she's getting?'

Long pause. Pursed lips. Iron plugged in to test. Eventually he said, 'She's never eaten much. I don't know. How should I know?'

Yvonne said, 'I'm giving you a few butterscotch, but mainly vanilla because I'm fed up with them. You won't get hungry. Well, *you* might, but they do fill you up. You want to get Eleanor on them as well, so she looks nice for the wedding photos. They save you dragging round Tesco's as well. In the future, you know, they'll do away with food altogether.'

Scott mooched in. He said, 'Are you getting me CD-ROMs for Christmas? You can get me Shadow-caster or Space Hulk or Underworld Seven, but not Young Scientist or anything sad like that.' Christmas. Eleanor's sorted. She needs stuff for St Lucia, but I hadn't even thought about what I'd get for Kayleigh and the other little mouth-breather. I have now though. A nice book. Maybe a nice Illustrated Children's Bible, with my special Christmas wishes written in, so he can't take it back and exchange it for Space Hulk.

Words between Eleanor and the bride, so Alec's feeling the squeeze. First, Elly has a very sketchy idea about St Lucia, except that it'll be far away from me and Birmingham, so she's in favour of it. Second, she really doesn't understand how unsuitable Doc Marten boots would be for someone who'll be posing under an archway of jacaranda with the happy couple. Nikki is thinking floating pastels; Eleanor's thinking new 501s and a black T-shirt. I gather they locked horns in Shipham's haber-dashery department on Saturday afternoon, and Alec just stood there, fingering his John Lewis store card. According to Eleanor, he's going to wear a white tuxedo, pink dress-shirt and a bow tie in parakeet green, which is a bit of a turnaround from when he married me. That time his suit was the same shade of grey as his face.

They say every bride deserves a day to remember. The thing was, we fixed the date because we thought I was pregnant, and I didn't find out I wasn't until I was on my way to the wedding. It was register office, but my mother had brought in heavy artillery to pound our dress standards position. To her way of thinking, a marriage entered into in a burgundy knickerbocker suit from Chelsea Girl carried no legal weight, so I wore a borrowed ivory satin empire line with a Juliet cap and a hushed-up unhappy history. There we all were, my dad and Philip in Burton suits bought specially, and Mum in a face that'd freeze hell, all squashed into a registrar's room the size of a phone booth. It was a good job I hadn't hired a crinoline and matching bridal parasol.

We had a finger buffet at the Glamis. That was my earliest sighting of scrambled-egg vol-au-vents. My dad got billyboy from Mum for taking his tie off after the toasts, but quietly, out the back, so Alec's people didn't think she was uncouth. Alec's people would never have thought any such thing. EPNS teaspoon for teaspoon our families were perfectly matched. That was the problem, Mum needed to be able to take up a stance.

If they'd had airs and graces, she could have played the dignified peasant; if they'd been riff-raff she could have risen graciously above them; either way she could have kept her distance. But as it was, they were exactly like us, so when Alec's Dad said, 'Muriel, you've got a smashing daughter, you must be very proud of her,' I could see her squirm.

Afterwards we had three nights at a hotel in Bournemouth and we had to have a twin-bedded room, because of a mix-up with the booking. Neither of us was that bothered; I was just happy to be married and not pregnant, and Alec's head was full of schemes. He always preferred money to sex. I don't suppose Nikki was even born then.

So here's the plan: shed a bit of avoirdupoids – because I want to, not because of anything Tonya said – get the Buf-Puf to work on certain lack-lustre areas, such as my entire body; and try to stop chewing my nails. Also to mug up on some opinions in the Sunday paper, so I appear to have a lively and interesting take on current affairs; fix the shower curtain; and give Hegarty an ultimatum. I want book deals. I want requests to open superstores. I want my own series on BBC2 and fully spongeable recipe cards with free ring-binder that will build into a magnificent collection you'll love to keep.

Tonya said, 'Well, my dear, I think you're ready. I'm going to put you in touch with Terence. Fifty-one, five eleven, divorced, no dependents, blue eyes, silver hair.'

I said, 'You didn't send him to see Mr Antony then?'

She gave me a taut shiny smile and gimlet eyes, folded her hands and leaned forward sincerely.

She said, 'May I say something, Elizabeth? Here at Crème de la Crème we take great pride in our standards; I'm sure you take pride in your work. And I see a very important part of our service as helping people to make the best of themselves. Now, one of the things we've learned after all these years in the business is that ladies with greying hair are very hard to place, even with the more mature gentlemen. Now, of course, we do get ladies who suggest that this is unfair, and what I have to say to them is this: fair has nothing to do with it. We're talking market forces, we're talking fierce competition. It's dog-eat-dog out there, unless you're Michelle Pfeiffer, and it

72

gets harder with every year that passes. There just aren't enough men to go round. He can take his pick. Hm? Get what he wants. And he wants you slim, he wants you fragrant, and he doesn't want you in lace-up shoes. That's the bottom line. Naming no names, we had a client in here, very successful professional lady, but her face was a stranger to night cream. She was a highly eligible lady in many respects and we really didn't want to lose her. I urged her to cleanse, tone and nourish, because it's the very least any of us can get away with, especially after thirty-five. Anyway, sadly, I wasn't able to persuade her and we had to let her go. One of our gentlemen who did meet her said if that was the kind of thing he should expect he was inclined to send off for a lovely young Filipino girl instead. But now you see *you* took my advice, and I can see a difference already. Another tip: try a lash tint; it's a very good way of making your eyes look bigger. And a few pointers about dates too, because let's face it, we all get rusty, don't we? And times change, I mean, dating isn't what it was in the sixties.'

Good, because I don't want to go to an air show and sit on a blanket with a man who gets moved to tears by the sight of a plane with cardboard wings, or watch him air-strum 'House of the Rising Sun' or argue with him about condoms in the back of a Hillman Imp.

'. . . The first few dates,' she said, 'should be kept sweet and light. Let him do all the work, let him decide where you go; just dress nicely, act nicely, peck him on the

73

cheek and go home, and don't ever mention seeing him again, all right? If it gets to the third date, then you can afford to open up a bit more, but remember, men love a good listener, and what I always say to my ladies with careers is this, "Don't ram it down his throat." I mean, no man wants to hear how brilliant you are. Am I right? A man needs to feel like a man. I know I'm old-fashioned but I make no apology. Where does all this feminist malarkey get you? I'll tell you: cauliflower cheese for one on a Saturday night. I mean, I see a lot of this in my business, this modern attitude that says it's all right for a lady to call up a gentleman or even ask him out. They say to me, "I have men working for me. I'm the equal of any man and it doesn't bother me to make the first move." But it bothers me, because I know it's a big mistake. If you don't make a man run after you he'll think you're not worth having, and if he doesn't think you're worth fighting for he's never going to pop the question, and that's what we're here for, isn't it?'

I said, 'Well I'd settle for the occasional dinner with any man who doesn't have a row of coloured biros in his top pocket.'

Tonya knew not of what I spoke.

'Of course, dinner,' she said. 'But a lot of ladies do themselves no favours over dinner. They talk too much, they argue, laugh too loud, sometimes they even offer to split the bill. They break every rule in the book and then they're on the phone to me. "Tonya, I liked him

74

but he never called." It's a sign of the times. Girls flashing their Mastercard around and asking men for their number. Take my advice, my dear, you just stick at that diet and let Terence do the rest. Now, what else can I tell you? He's a Virgo and he lists his interests as theatre, dining out, and orienteering. He did explain that one to me but I can't quite remember what it is. Anyway, that'll be something you can ask him about.'

Uh-oh, I think I might know what it is. I think I'm getting a phantom whiff of old running shoes. Anyway, I've now taken violently against anything connected with Tonya, so when I meet him, and I'm definitely going to meet him because Tonya's cashed my non-refundable £250, Terence could be in for a rough ride.

The news of the moment from Glenville Close is that you can no longer buy Min furniture polish, and Ronald Reagan's first wife has become worryingly frail.

She said, 'What's happening about Christmas?'

I said, 'You're going to Philip and Yvonne's.'

'Yes,' she said, 'I know what I'm doing. What are you doing? Are you having company?' When we were kids, *having company* ranked with getting your teeth drilled, or having to take threadworm medicine because your mum had seen you scratching. Fortunately, company only happened about twice a year, when Aunty Edie and Uncle Cyril foisted themselves on us for Sunday tea, and once every five years when Aunty Phyllis came home from Argentina wearing scent.

For Edie and Cyril the windows were cleaned and the teacloths were given an extra boil, but for Aunty Phyllis the whole house was scrubbed down with hard green soap and hot water. We didn't want her going back to

Buenos Aires and putting it about that things weren't being kept up to scratch. *UK Grime Shock For Corned Beef Woman.*

After the wash-down we were all kept under close observation, lest we roam around and destroy all Mum's hard work. It had to be done; without it there was no telling what havoc we might have wrought, opening doors without using the knob, coming down stairs heavy-footed and creating dust.

By the time we got back from Sunday school the household had moved from red alert to flashing blue lights. Dad was made to shave – there was more to that than met the eye; some sort of long-running niggle between Edie and Mum over who'd get Cyril and who'd get our Dad. He had to shave to show that he'd been a good catch and not the kind of man to sit around on a Sunday afternoon with bristles, which he was. We loved his bristles, me and Philip; we used to beg him to scratch us.

He'd shave in the kitchen, taking care not to splatter on the cakes left cooling on a wire rack, and then he'd stand around in his vest and braces, not allowed his clean shirt until the last minute, on call for manly duties such as unscrewing the top off a new jar of beetroot. My duties were helping spread the best tablecloth and arranging the good cups and saucers so all the handles pointed the same way. These jobs were women's mysteries. Philip's job was to read his comic quietly and not scuff his shoes.

Company. Uncle Cyril doing his trick with a

handkerchief and a penny, and Aunty Edie saying how we'd grown and what a pity it was that the boys always got the wavy hair and the good eyelashes, and the whole thing grinding to a silent halt once the tea things were washed and dried.

Aunty Phyllis was better, but I only remember her coming twice. She was the one who'd gone away to foreign parts, where you couldn't get HP sauce or Omo washing-powder. When I was five and she wrote to say she was coming, I expected her to have a black face like the fuzzy-wuzzies in my *Story of the World in Pictures*. I was ten the next time she came and I'd looked up Argentina in my atlas.

Phyllis was fast. It was never said, but you didn't need to be a rocket scientist to work it out. For one thing, she'd gone out there engaged to Harry, who was with the bank, chucked him and married Osbaldo who was in beef; for another thing, she didn't wear stockings. The skin on her shins was brown and papery, but her face was pale and nice, and she wore big clip-on earrings that she let me try on, and peep-toe shoes.

I remember a fight over money. Dad had got down from the table after tea, which he was allowed to do so long as he didn't fall asleep. Phyllis tried to give my mother money; Mum refused it. It was pushed back and forth in a great wad of fivers and then it just lay there in no man's land between the milk jug and the Viennese Fancies, until a final skirmish when Phyllis had her coat on, ready to go, and stuffed the money into my hand as she kissed me goodbye, and my mother, trained by MI5 to spot stealthy drops, shoved it through the taxi window and said, 'I'm sure there are some little foreign orphans who'd be glad of it.'

Aunty Phyllis didn't make it for tea the year I was fifteen. We got a letter from Uncle Osbaldo to say she'd had peritonitis in somewhere called Fatima, and a photograph of the floral tributes and all their staff lined up, looking sad in black armbands. When I saw that I realized that not being able to get Omo probably hadn't had too much of an impact on Phyllis's life.

I said, 'I'm sure Yvonne's told you, Eleanor's going to the Caribbean with Alec, to be there for his wedding, and I'm coming to Yvonne and Philip's for lunch, so I shall see you there. I shan't stay late though, I've got other things arranged.' Liar, liar, pants on fire.

She said, 'I'm giving everybody vouchers. I don't know what people want these days. It's all computers and unisex. Should I put Eleanor's in the post? Will she get it? Will they take vouchers over there? Fancy going all that way. Is it a coloured he's marrying?'

I said, 'No need to send it, she can have it when she gets back. You'll get a shock when you see Yvonne, I'd say she's lost a stone at least.'

'Yes,' she said, 'Jane Wyman's down to seventy pounds. She was marvellous in *Johnny Belinda*.'

I arranged to meet Terence in the Windsor Bar at the Midland Hotel. He said he'd be wearing a blazer, and there he was, reading the *Evening News* and sipping at a half, looking dead nonchalant. I'd been doing a bit of advance work on Comforting Winter Casseroles and hadn't had time to actually eat anything, apart from a couple of onion rings while I was at the chopping board, so after two gin and tonics my insides were playing variations on a rococo theme. I suggested dinner, which is a capital offence in Tonya's book, and also, because she'd put my back up with all that stuff about painting your nails and not wearing Hush Puppies, I'd turned up pretty well *au naturel*.

Terence was quite attractive. Slim and wiry. I prefer a bit more padding, but it's not important.

We managed to find the worst Indian in town. He had gristle and sinew moghlai with bright orange rice. I had a shoe-leather jalfrezi and got an angry flush spreading up my throat and cheeks. There was a mirror on the wall behind Terence, so I had plenty of opportunity to notice that it wasn't a good look. I said, 'I understand you like the theatre?'

He said, 'Oh, yes. I saw *Starlight Express* a year or two back. Have you seen it at all? It's a marvellous show. I'd like to see it again some day. Doesn't come cheap though, going to a show.'

I said, 'No? I haven't been in a long time. When you work in show business like I do, you find you want to relax away from bright lights and big egos.' I had to squeeze it in. He was on his second half of Kaliber and he hadn't mentioned my being famous or anything.

He said, 'Oh, yes, Tonya did tell me. I can't say I've ever seen you; I don't watch much telly these days. I find my orienteering keeps me pretty busy actually.'

I smiled one of my good-sort smiles when I realized he hadn't taped the show and watched it avidly when he knew he was going to meet me – that's what I would have done.

I liked his aftershave, though, and I liked the idea of having a date, so I asked him about his orienteering. That lit him up 150 watts.

He said, 'I should warn you, get me started on orienteering and we could be here all night. Great sport. I can't imagine where my life would be today if I hadn't discovered it. It originated in Sweden, you know? I got started in seventy-four. Friend of mine said, "Come along,

81

Tez. Give it a try," and I've never looked back. And, of course, these days I'm involved at federation level. I've got my spare room kitted out as an office, so there's all the paper work as well as keeping in training. You should try it, you'd love it. It's like a car rally, only you're on foot, and you're relying on your own fitness. Fresh air. Using your brain. Great. And it's very character-building; a lot of people don't realize that. I'll give you an example: you're running along, going well, looking for your next marker, and then you see somebody else going in completely the opposite direction, and you think, Have I slipped up? Or you're rattling along and you get to a spot and there's half a dozen people milling round because the marker's not where they thought it'd be, and they're all shouting the odds; one thinks one thing, somebody else thinks the opposite. What do you do? I'll tell you. You've got to have the discipline to stick to your guns. You've got to trust your own judgement and not waste time standing round having a mothers' meeting. It's just you out there with your map and your compass and your safety whistle. You're on your own, that's the bottom line. Do you run at all?'

I did run. I think it was 1961, first hockey lesson of the autumn term and Olive Oyle Satterthwaite made me play right wing and screamed, 'Run, Clarke. Run, girl. You're not out for a country walk.'

Some people aren't built to run, same as some people aren't wired up to play chess. And it's not an imperative of human existence after all; it's not like breathing. Back in the caves we wouldn't all have had to be runners; we wouldn't all have been hunters, out there dodging the sabre-toothed tigers, trying to bring home a leg of bison. Some of us would have stayed behind and done decorative things with stains made from woodland berries. But try telling that to a runner.

Satterthwaite was my nemesis. I never managed to get any useful stuff on her, and nearly everything she made us do involved intercepting a ball in flight. Even when the weather was too severe for us to go outside, we had to do team races with netballs and beanbags, and no one ever picked me for their team. Someone ended up having to have me, and then they'd say, 'Aaah-uh, Mi-iss. Do we have to?'

It's hard, that, when you're brilliant at everything else. You suffer both ways: despised for always getting merit marks for your essays and chemistry tests, and despised for never scoring a rounder. If you didn't have other advantages, like stealth and cunning, you could end up without a friend in the world.

I made light of my not running. I was thinking that if things worked out between us, there'd be other things I could do while Terence was orienteering. I could drive his support vehicle or be at the finish with a packed lunch or something. I was planning a big future with a man who owned five different styles of running shoe, because that's how you get when you're nearly fifty and the men you used to snog on Rolleston Rec are dropping with coronaries or marrying girls who could be your daughter.

Then I did it. Picked up the bill. I don't know how it happened. I was laughing and nodding too much, trying to show it was cool with me if he wasn't bowled over by my fame and beauty, making out he was delighting me with his every word, and I just reached out and picked it up.

He didn't put up a fight. He feigned going for his wallet and then he said, 'Oh, right, a liberated lady. Ta very much.' He didn't mention seeing me again either. He just said, 'Well, it's been very nice. I shall have to watch out for you on the goggle-box.' So I'm thirty quid down for some little ferret in a blazer from Top Man, and I'm going to get bell, book and candle from Tonya first thing Monday.

To Mass. I went early, to have time to reconnoitre and get a good seat. You don't really need to, of course; that's one of the things I like about Catholics. They come late, wander around, kneel, stand, wave to friends, leave early. But those C of E habits die hard: bums on seats by 10.55 and don't even think of budging until the end.

Himself was there, feeding coins into the candle-money tin, so I swerved away and just got to my knees where I could watch him and Our Lady of Good Counsel could watch me. Beautiful clean hair, strong white hands. I think he could be a teacher – the old-fashioned kind who talks quietly and gets a load of grief from the big boys. I think he lives alone, with a gas fire and a two-cup teapot, and dreams of what might have been if he'd only met a good woman and seized the day.

I said, 'Hail Mary, full of grace' and a whole string of Glory Bes to try and concentrate my mind, but life kept intruding. Whether to have a butterscotch-flavoured drink and vitamin-enriched biscuit bar for dinner or a toasted sourdough sandwich of thinly sliced rare beef, anointed with caramelized garlic and basil in oil. Decisions, decisions.

I decided: the beef sandwich. And I wouldn't tail him this time. When you're investigating someone, you need to hold back sometimes, in case they're getting that feeling of being watched. Sometimes you've got to be willing to wait, or let stuff come to you, and I am. So I didn't wait for Father Mullen to say, '*Ite, missa est.*' As soon as he started up about spare seats on a coach trip to Walsingham, I shot out of the back door fast.

The sun was in my eyes, low in the sky, and I had to keep leaning into the bitter wind and dabbing my nose with Andrex. He must have overtaken me on his bike without my seeing him, because when I got to the Nip-In, to buy mustard and eggs and alphabetti spaghetti for Eleanor, he was there already, paying Surinder to put an advert in the window for a fortnight. Except that Surinder didn't; not straight off. He left the postcard by the till, turned over so I couldn't even try to read it, because Meera started yelling at him from the back of the shop, and when Meera tells Surinder to jump he only pauses long enough to ask, 'How high?'

I hung about, feigning deep interest in gardening magazines, hoping he'd come back out to the till and put the card in the window, but he was too busy portering cartons of Cheesy Wotsits, and when Meera took my money she didn't even notice the card. I had to go back three times, strolling by casually. It was starting to get dark when my big moment finally arrived. The moment when I saw his handwriting, and found out his address.

Baby Burco wash boiler, as new   £35
Snipe kayak, bit ripped   £75

7 Ryedale Court, evenings.

No name, no number, and the writing was a bit blobby, but still, a legitimate opportunity for me to drive round to Ryedale Court and open the bidding. Not straight away though; I figured I should leave it a day or two. Call it a gamble, but I didn't foresee a stampede.

Louie said, 'Tiffany, home moves and family developments are on the way.' He told me he'd seen her buying a pregnancy-test kit in the chemist's at Five Ways.

He said, 'Your mood may be unsettled, but Venus meeting Jupiter in your sign can only mean an opportunity for happiness. Be open-minded and take extra care with your health. Now, look here, I've got curlies sprouting out of my nostrils all of a sudden. I look like I've been snorting Gro-Rite lawn tonic. Can you get rid of them for me? I think I might be getting some in my ears as well. Will I need an anaesthetic?'

She said, 'That's all right, Louie, I'll trim them. I did Jasper Carrot's when he was on. But that's really incredible, what you said about moving house and everything, because my Neil's been saying it's the right time to sell. He was saying last night he'd like us to get somewhere with a bit more garden.'

Kim said, 'You can have ours. We have to get an extra

man in in the autumn just to keep it clear of leaves, and I never go out there now there's a hole in the ozone layer. Tiffany, I'd like you to finish my make-up please, before you go poking around up people's noses. I'm not a prejudiced person, but I'm afraid I've read too many horror stories about mucous membranes.' *TV Gay In Shared Tweezer Health Scare.*

Louie said, 'No, Kim. You're quite right. Anyway, we always practice safe make-up, don't we, Tiff?'

Meredith liked my filo parcels and the little crostini, but he wasn't sure about the filling for the baby potatoes. He didn't think the Midlands were ready for lumpfish caviar. A bit of projection going on there, I'd say. I've had a lot of trouble with him over offal as well.

Kim said, 'Hello and welcome. We've got another great programme for you this morning. Valerie Tobin's back with us, and I know a lot of you are really looking forward to her Countdown to a Slimmer Christmas. Valerie'll be pleased to answer your questions on dieting during this difficult time of year. Our lines are open now, so if you'd like to talk to Valerie later, call us on this number coming up on your screen right now. Also today, we've got tips on how to revitalize those bowls of pot pourri that are gathering dust, we shall be talking to *Flying Doctor* heart-throb Damian Dunne, who's just flown in to start rehearsals for the role of Prince Zanziboo in *Aladdin*, and we have your stars for the week. So sit down with a cup of coffee and decide nothing until you've heard what the week ahead promises. And In the Kitchen, Lizzie will be looking at easy-to-make party nibbles. But first' — rearrange face into expression of suitable gravity — 'the growing problem of Britain's homeless. What kind of Christmas can they look forward to? I'm talking this morning to Wanda Relphs from the charity, Bleak Midwinter. Wanda, tell us what Bleak Midwinter aims to do for the homeless and gardenless.'

One of the cameramen laughed out loud, and Wanda looked a bit startled, but her mind was really on saying her piece. Kim kept her compassionate nod going at a steady rhythm, head on one side. 'Something that concerns us all, I'm sure,' she said, winding it up, 'and if you feel you'd like to do something to help, maybe volunteer a little of your time or make a donation, you can call this number: 600 6000. So that's 121 1212 if you have a slimming question for Valerie, and 600 6000 if you'd like to help the homeless and gardenless.'

Stuart tried to come in fast over the laughter. He said, 'And stay with us, because after the break we'll be In the Kitchen with Lizzie Partridge.'

She was out of her chair as soon as we were off the air, and screaming, 'Get those fucking jackasses off my show. Who was it? Come on, who was it? Where's Meredith? Just thank your lucky stars I'm a fucking professional, that's all. There's a good many would go to pieces. This is a live show, do I have to remind you? Do I?'

Alison hurried poor Wanda away. Stuart whispered something to Kim.

She said, 'What? Are you crazy? Do you think I don't know what I said? Excuse me, Stuart. I mean, I've been in this business a long time. Don't tell me what I said. I have perfect recall. Nothing gets past me, nothing. Ask Tiffany. And get me a fucking paracetamol, somebody. Right now. I mean, does anyone around here actually know what the fuck they're doing?'

Valerie was miked up and ready to go in a scarlet satin and Lycra catsuit with acrylic ermine trim. She cast her calorie-counting eye over my dates stuffed with Roquefort, butter and brandy and said, 'Who eats stuff like this any more? Still swimming against the tide, I see, Lizzie? Still letting out those waistbands?'

I said, 'Yep, and I see you're still scraping your bony shins up the bestseller lists.' I didn't say anything about her having a face like a komodo dragon; I'm saving that for when I've got a really appreciative audience. I like being on the same show as Valerie. The sight of her scrawny neck makes me really purr to the camera. And Meredith likes it when I lick my fingers.

The phone lines were jammed. The faithful queueing up to get their resolve stiffened.

'Keep a photo on your fridge door,' she told Pat from Coleshill, 'a photo of someone really fat and flabby. And keep a box of carrot sticks ready prepared as well, in case the photo isn't enough to stop you opening that fridge door and snacking.'

She said it still wasn't too late to fit into that gorgeous little black dress, if you were really determined. Grapefruit and black coffee for breakfast, cottage cheese and pineapple for lunch, steak and salad for dinner, and if eating out was absolutely unavoidable the things to remember were, keep your hands out of the bread basket, push away the butter, sip slowly on one glass of dry white wine, and slip an apple into your evening bag in case someone tries to tempt you with a slice of Mississippi mud pie.

Kim said, 'We seem to have lost Sandra from Bartley Green, but she wants a flatter stomach for her hubby's company dinner on the fifteenth. Any special tips on tums, Valerie?'

'Yes, Kim,' she said. 'My new exercise video, *More Toning with Tobin*, is in the shops, price nine pounds ninety-nine, and it deals with all the problem areas: tummy bulge, BTM overhang, jodhpur thighs, upper-arm wobble. It's a completely new workout with lots of lovely new exercises set to Latin American tunes, and it comes with a special-offer coupon for my new range of Spandex leisurewear. This lovely festive leotard I'm wearing this morning is an example of how you can look great and feel great, even while you're exercising.'

Kim said, 'And very affordable too. I've been browsing through the catalogue and I've been very impressed. This one you're modelling for us this morning, Valerie, you could almost wear this to a party.'

So Kim's obviously joined the payroll of the Valerie Tobin fat-free Spandex mega-empire.

Louie said, 'Give me one of those date and Roquefort jobbies, you dark-haired temptress. I think I've just pulled. The handsome but wicked Prince Zanziboo's asked me round to his dressing-room to see his snaps of scenic sub-tropical Queensland. I told him it was a place I'd always planned to visit. I lied.'

I went round to Ryedale last night. Washed my hair, put a slick of Vaseline under my eyes, like Tiff showed me, wore my red chenille jumper, but there was no one home. I left a note with my name and number, to say I was interested in buying, but there was something rabid hurling itself at the letter-box between snarls, so I don't suppose the message reached its destination. Funny, I'd been prepared for him to have an unhealthy relationship with a Siamese cat, or perhaps a small caged finch, but I hadn't bargained on a dog.

I've been feeling a bit off; my skin's crawling. I stripped off and had a good look in the mirror. I couldn't see the ten thousand giant ants that were proceeding in a southerly direction down my back, but I know for sure they were there.

It's always a bad time for me when I've got a long break between shows. I need stuff to work on, like researching prospective lovers and perfecting my three-chocolate terrine. I need someone to talk to at nights. I need someone to talk to.

Tonya called and she didn't tell me off about paying for dinner, so Terence evidently didn't blab. She said he's got a big competition coming up, and hasn't really got time to see anyone for a while. Who cares? I bet he keeps athlete's foot remedy on his night table. Tonya asked whether I would like to speak to Bernard, forty-eight, divorced and keen on motoring and the finer things in life, only it might have to be after Christmas because he's visiting his children in Winnipeg.

One o'clock and no signs of life from Eleanor. Imagine going all the way to Winnipeg and finding they're still in bed.

We're supposed to be going shopping to buy her a swimsuit and sun cream because they leave for St Lucia tomorrow, but all I've seen of her so far is one grungy foot sticking out from under the duvet. I collected up a few choice items while I was in there. Long-lost dinner plates, cola cans, Marmite crusts, the telephone directory, KitKat wrappers, mugs growing penicillin. Tiptoeing round, because you never know what you might stand on – the surface may look like socks and sweatshirts, but the next layer down could be razor wire. Anyway, I disturbed her. Scowling out at me through mascara build-up.

I said, 'Eleanor, it's afternoon. What time are you going to be ready to go out?'

I was giving her the kid-glove treatment. I don't want her bitching to Alec about what a tough time I give her. Don't want the three of them sitting round with their pineapple daiquiris talking about how nagging can be a symptom of deep personal unhappiness.

She disappeared back under the covers, wriggling around, trying to escape from the daylight. She said, 'Orright, orright, I'm coming. I'm just tired, orright?'

How is this possible? How can a girl aged sixteen and three-quarters have less energy than a woman of forty-eight who's had mastitis, gallstones and a very bad case of shingles? What am I missing? She was breast-fed. She had fluoride for her teeth and vitamin drops in her Farex. Fresh air, pesticide-free apples and no telly after *Jackanory*. And now she lies there like she's in a Limehouse opium den. My mother blames the Americans. Nothing specific on the charge sheet, you understand. No forensic evidence, as such. Just this gut feeling she's had since about 1942.

Actually, for once I don't think she's that far off the mark. I think Eleanor's torpor could be to do with central heating, and I suppose we got that from the Americans. You never wanted to stay in bed when I was sixteen. A sheet and one thin slippy-slidey quilt was all that stood between you and ice on the inside of the window. You wanted to be up, dressed and hugging the fire. And even if it wasn't cold, you wanted to escape from the damp patch on the wallpaper and the sound of the Hoover

Carpet-master sucking and whining at the gap under your bedroom door.

I waited till three and then went without her. I didn't slam the door, and I let the handbrake off and rolled out onto the road before I started the engine. No sense in waking the sleeping princess, much better to slip away quietly and stay out till the shops are closed, then come home and enjoy her indignation.

I hadn't really thought how close to Christmas it's getting. I had to wait for a space in the multi-storey, and wait for a lift to the shopping level, and then there it was, yule-tide, right in my face. They had boxes of steam-heated hair rollers piled up in Fraser's, labelled 'Ideal Gift' and 'Mary's Boy Child' on the PA system, and a girl in a khaki uniform standing by the escalator with a megaphone shouting, 'Standing on the right, walking on the left,' over and over. To think, all this started with a little baby in a manger.

I bought everything I needed. When Elly was younger I used to start in September, getting little things I thought she'd like. But I'm a one-stop shopper now. I bought a lockable diary for Kayleigh, *Treasure Island* for Scott, a bottle of Baileys for Yvonne, Bristol Cream chocolates for Mum, a Patsy Kline CD for Philip, a big box of white candles for Christmas Eve, and a silk waistcoat from the craft market for Louie, in burgundy, silver and black, and a pull-on latex mask of the Queen, because he's really good at doing her voice. He can do Daffy Duck as well.

I relented a bit over Eleanor, and got her some banana-hair putty and jelly-baby bath foam, in case she remembers about it being Christmas. Then I had a stale cheese baguette and tea from a pot that wouldn't pour, and went to the Sacred Heart, sat in the dark and had a bloody good cry. Don't know why.

I might as well have come home to an empty house. She hadn't put a match to the fire or turned the lamps on. She was curled up in her cardigan, picking at the spot on her chin and talking to Emma or Gemma or some other know-nothing bubble brain.

I wasn't searching her suitcase. I just thought I'd slip the things I'd bought her between her clothes, for her to find later. I really didn't want to find that she'd packed T-shirts that would fail the Window Test for Whites, and a Polaroid of Gavin wearing nothing but his baseball cap.

She said, 'Is there dinner?'

I said, 'If you'd got your backside out of bed before sunset we could have gone for a quick Chinese after we'd finished shopping.'

She started eating gherkins from the jar. She said, 'God, who wants to go shoving round Fraser's? Brum's a dump. I can't stick the place.'

I said, 'Yeah. Shoving round Fraser's the week before Christmas buying things I can't afford for people I don't even like is certainly one of my favourite ways of spending an afternoon. Still, there wasn't the same pressure on you, was there? You know, what with you being happy to fly to the Caribbean without a swimsuit and everything?'

She said, 'These yoghurts should have been chucked. They're all best before December second. God, there's never nothing to eat in this house.'

I said, 'So are you ready? Everything packed?' *Porn Pic Swoop: Local Girl Held.*

She said, 'I can get stuff at the airport, Dad said. Dad said when you're travelling you should take half as much luggage and twice as much money. Am I getting money off you? Can I sell you the voucher Nana sent me?'

Alec picked her up at about nine. They've got an early start in the morning. He didn't come to the door so I didn't have to work out how to convey my sincere good wishes as he sets out on a disastrous marriage to a girl who is younger than my transistor radio. I kept expecting Mr Ryedale Court to phone and arrange for me to view his Baby Burco, but he kept not doing it.

I watched some dire old sitcom with men in flared trousers and kipper ties. Finished the gherkins. Also two out-of-date crunch-corner yoghurts and a packet of Jaffa cakes. Lay awake then with an ache in my chest. I hadn't felt like that since the night Eleanor was born, and I wanted to keep her with me, but they took her away to the nursery to give her a bottle because I was only her stupid mother and didn't I know I wouldn't have any milk for three days? It might have been the gherkins this time though.

I said, 'I've come about the wash boiler. I left a note the other night.'

He didn't recognize me. He said, 'It's thirty-five pounds.'

Funny, he wasn't at all mellifluously Irish with sad eyes and a bashful smile, which was kind of what I was banking on. He was just a regular Brummie and his house smelled of old pancakes.

I said, 'Can I see it?'

He said, 'It's out the back, I shall have to unlock.' He said it like you might say, 'I shall have to crawl across this minefield.' And he was gone some time, fetching the key, which left me trapped between his bike and a corgi that kept levitating towards my throat and yapping the scale of C major.

He took me through the kitchen. He'd been sitting at a table in there, marking maths books, so I was right about one thing, at least. The boiler was outside, in a lean-to, with ancient electric fires and bundles of old newspapers and polythene bags of silver paper.

He said, 'It's never been used. It was my mother's, but she preferred her old one, so she never did use this one. I got your note. You shouldn't give your particulars to strangers. You want to be more careful.'

I said, 'It's bigger than I wanted.'

He said, 'They only come in this size. What do you want it for?'

I murmured something about steamed puddings, and that I'd have to think it over.

He said, 'You won't get anything smaller. They don't even make them any more. Thirty pounds. Is your husband waiting outside?'

I said he was expecting me.

He said, 'Twenty-five pounds and I'll deliver it. I can bring it round on my handlebars. What street did you say?'

I said, 'No need. I've got my car outside. Twenty pounds?'

He said, 'Done. What about the kayak?'

So there goes another dream down the U-bend. I shan't be sipping Bushmills and sailing to Byzantium by the glow of a turf fire, after all, and I haven't even got a spare fantasy lined up. Nothing to fall back on except the confidential executive register at Crème de la Crème Introductions for the Discerning.

His corgi was called Bambi. Disappointments don't come much crueller than that. And the boiler hasn't got a plug. Also, the invisible marching ants are back.

I made this thing for the table. Pomegranates and physalis, sprayed gold, with fake snowberries and some purple sage from the garden. Then I lit the candles.

Louie arrived with a basket over his arm like Little Red Riding Hood. Clementines with their leaves on, in dark-blue tissue-paper; quails eggs, hard boiled in their speckly shells; a wedge of mountain Gorgonzola, and a bottle of Spätlese, cold from his fridge.

He said, 'Where's your Christmas tree?'

He made me fetch Elly's old plastic Scotch pine from the top of the wardrobe. He followed me up there and got showered with dust, but he didn't seem to notice. He was hopping around and talking ten to the dozen. I think Louie likes Christmas Eve.

He said, 'You can't not have a tree. Bags I'm in charge. And get me all the decorations. I don't want you holding back the tat. I wasn't allowed a tree when I was with Chas. We had a tasteful twig with white satin ribbons from that lifestyle shop near Seven Dials, and every time I put my Woolies fairy on it he took her off. Have you got a fairy? Now here's what I thought: have some grub, well, do the tree first, then have some grub. Go to Mass, then come back, and have prezzies and pud with this fabulous wine I brought you.'

So that's what we did. He got the fairy lights working and loaded the tree, while I told him about Terence and Mr Ryedale Court, and there wasn't a bauble left in the box when he'd finished. Then we had smoked eel with brown bread and horseradish, and some fat sweet mussels, sizzled on the half shell with butter and almonds. Louie was in charge of drinks. A shot of Armagnac over ice with a twist of orange. He just kept them coming.

He said, 'Why are you putting yourself through all this? You must stop it at once. Tell Tonyonyonya you want your money back. Tell her you've got herpes. She'll drop you like a shot. I'll find you a man, if that's what you really want.'

I said I thought it was, because I've got all the other things like a great job and a child and a house and a car.

He said, 'And you've got your health and freedom and an electric juicer. Could be you're better off on your own though. Not like me. You know how I am: not contented unless I've got somebody blunting my razor and tapping me for my last tenner. You're more self-contained. Why don't you just go out on dates and keep your independence?'

I said, 'What do you mean, just go out on dates? That's my point, I don't get dates; I get disappointments and men in white socks. And everyone keeps telling me there's a lot to be said for being on your own, but that's just big talk because they still go home and snuggle up with these men they say we're better off without, and they haven't got to spend Christmas Day at our Philip's.'

'No,' he said, '*they* probably have got to spend Christmas with gruesome rellies, *you're* the one who's free as a bird. You could have done anything you wanted. Come with me to Cheltenham.'

How could I? Yvonne was expecting me.

He said, 'Lizzie, I don't think you know what you want, but I will keep a lookout for nice men. I'll find one for you and one for me.'

I said, 'What star sign would you recommend?'

He said, 'Amex, the platinum-card bearer. Now, are you quite sure you want to go to midnight Mass with an unrepentant sodomite and all that? Because if I get turned into a pillar of salt or spontaneously combust or something, it could really ruin your Christmas.'

The church was too crowded for me to see whether Mr Ryedale was there. He wouldn't have known me, because he never looked at my face, but I still didn't want to see him. I didn't want to be reminded.

I'd left apples baking with rum and nutmeg and muscovado sugar. The smell of them met us on the doorstep and we had them with Louie's wine. Then I gave him his waistcoat and his mask and he put them both on and did his Queen voice, and said, 'It gives me great pleasure . . .' and presented me with a brass sundial inscribed 'Grow Old With Me, The Best Is Yet To Be'. He said, 'It was this or a replica of a bit of Michelangelo's David, only I couldn't get the bit I thought you'd like. They'd only got ears left, stacks of ears, so the sundial it was. Now, kissy kissy because I've got to be off. I'm due in Cheltenham at Strange Cousin Ralph's by lunchtime and I want to check out the Gaslight Club on my way home.'

There's nowhere quite so empty as the place Louie just left.

Philip had driven up to fetch Mum after the Leccy Board offices had closed, so she was well dug-in by Christmas morning, playing the abjectly grateful guest, refusing the chair nearest the fire, putting up with the faces on the TV screen being bright orange. The good part of it is she doesn't insist on helping in the kitchen because she doesn't understand ceramic hobs.

When we were kids, Christmas morning was like the dawn before a battle. She was up at six in a new apron and her front hair still in curlers. Her mission was to get the turkey into the oven, to steal a march on the neighbours before the gas pressure dropped and left you with your sprouts done but your meat still pink. Dad was allowed a lie-in till seven, because men were neither use nor ornament in the making of a roast dinner, and we had our parcels to open up in our room, to keep all the mess in one place. I had to help Philip. He never opened anything until I told him he could.

By the time Dad was up, the fire was lit, potatoes peeled, and the place had had a quick do round with the Ewbank. He had a dash of whisky in his first cup of tea, and pork pie with mustard pickles, which has to be the nastiest breakfast ever invented, but he seemed to like it, and after that he was really in party mood. We brought our presents down to show him what he'd bought us, and then we were allowed on the table with our colouring books till twelve – Philip always went outside the lines. Dad looked at his new Giles' cartoon book and Mum kept her eye on the turkey and any troop movements in the street, such as Aunty Jean's brothers arriving on a motor bike and sidecar, and the Liversedges going off to their married daughter's in Tennyson Drive. She never sat down in those days.

She was reading her library book when I arrived. Kayleigh was upstairs singing along with Whitney Houston. Scott was playing Lethal Enforcers II.

She said, 'You've been left all on your own then? Now you know what's it's like when your family's all gone. You'll soon be like me: nobody to talk to but the four walls.'

I said, 'You've never been on your own at Christmas. Anyway, women usually finish up on their own. How many do you know that have still got husbands alive?'

She said, 'I could have a fall, or a mini-stroke. I could lie there for days. Mrs Sanderson's got a button she can press.'

I said, 'Do you want a button?'

She didn't. I might just get her one anyway.

Yvonne had run amok in Freezacenters. She said, 'I got two boneless turkey roasts with stuffing, all the veggies, mince pies, brandy custard, king-prawn coronet with Marie Rose sauce, party-size tiramisu, crackers, Pepsi, dustbin sacks, tea-bags and bleach for the drains, pickles, ham, and a couple of squirters of cream, and I was in and out in twenty minutes. Did you want to do something? I thought you might want to do something fancy?'

I said, 'I brought these little oranges with their leaves on. Louie got them in London.'

She said, 'As long as they haven't got any creepy-crawlies on them. Did I tell you I might be selling time-shares? Costa Dorada. I've got an interview. The basic's not brilliant, but you get really good commission, and they send you out there for training courses. Did Eleanor get off all right? Serviettes, that's what you can do; fold the serviettes into something fancy.'

Philip had bought her a cordless lawn edger. I said, 'Should I take him outside and beat him up or do you want to do it yourself?'

She said, 'No, leave him. It don't matter. It was what he wanted, only I'd already paid out for an Arran jumper for him from the wool shop when he told me, so I said to get it and call it his present to me. I don't mind. I told him he can get me the diamond tarara next Christmas.'

★

112

When it was time to eat, Kayleigh couldn't hear us calling her, so Yvonne turned the power off and then she came out of her room to say her stereo was broken. Scott had had too much chocolate and didn't want to leave his game. Mum said, 'Somebody'll have to give me a hand up out of this chair.' Philip levered her up and she farted the Trumpet Voluntary all the way into the dinette. At least she didn't apologize. I can see there is an up side to being an old lady.

Kayleigh said, 'I in't wearing a paper hat. I in't eating greens.'

I wondered what Elly was doing. My lovely, bright, funny Elly.

I said, 'Phil, remember the Christmas Uncle Dennis said he could get us a bird wholesale? And he ran in with it and ran straight out again, and when Mum took it out of the bag it had 'UNFIT FOR HUMAN CONSUMPTION' stamped on it and it smelled soapy where he'd tried to scrub it off? And Dad had to go crawling round to Ledbetter's and plead for an old cockerel or anything they'd got left in the back of the shop?'

Mum said, 'It was just a misunderstanding. Anyway, going back over things all the time. What's the sense harking back? People don't want to hear all about that. Take no notice of her.'

Philip said, 'I think I might remember it.'

Yvonne had a slice of turkey and lots of gravy. She said, 'What did you get up to last night?' The ants were on the move again, down my scalp and neck, but I concentrated on telling her about going to church with Louie.

She said, 'What, at the catlick place? Are you allowed? I wish I'd known, I'd have come with you. I love the carols and everything. And wait till I tell Big Rita who you went with. She loves him. She says he's always spot on with her stars. It don't bother her that he's . . . you know . . .? Well it don't bother me really. You could have brought him with you today. You never bring anybody round.'

Mum rifted, sherry, sprouts, disapproval. Scott kicked Kayleigh under the table.

She said, 'I watched my stars last week. I'm to expect an exciting reunion, but I mustn't take my health for granted.'

I said, 'Louie didn't do a show last week; they bumped him over to make room for the Queen Mother's operation.'

'No,' she said, 'not your lot, the other side.'

Yvonne said, 'The one they've got doing the Lottery now; he's like that as well. There's even MPs. It don't bother me. Are you too hot?'

I was. The ants were wearing thermal socks and my blouse was sticking between my shoulder blades.

Philip said, 'Nancy boy,' and Scott said, 'Who is, Dad? Is he a shirt-lifter? Dad? Is he coming here?'

Mum said, 'Your face is bright red, Elizabeth. We get nicer horoscopes on our side.'

Sky TV Geminis Escape April Health Hitch.

Kayleigh said, 'Where's your girl?' She wanted to hear all about the wedding. She said, 'Is she allowed high heels, your girl? I am.'

Scott leaned across and said, 'Is he a bum bandit, that man? Is he a fudge-packer?' and the plates were passed politely up to Yvonne for scraping and clearing away.

Mum said, 'Your nana used to be a biscuit packer when your dad and Aunty Elizabeth were little, and an egg grader. Do you remember, Philip? Do you remember the big bags I used to bring home?'

I do. We were broken-biscuit millionaires, but so was nearly every other family in the street, so it didn't count for much.

Kayleigh latched on to me for the afternoon, showing me the photos of the five times she's been a bridesmaid and the clothes she's picked out from Empire Stores new spring catalogue. The telly went back on at three. You could have fried an egg on it by the time I left, about eight. I helped Yvonne make a dent in her bottle of Baileys. She said, 'I could live on this stuff. Did I tell you about the time-share thing? Did I ask you if you know anybody who wants a settee, second-hand? It's got to go. Look, it shows every mark. I thought fifty pounds, if you know of anybody.'

I never know how to say goodbye to my mother. I think it's because she doesn't participate. She just stands there, soaking up all your lies about how nice it's been and all your wild promises to drive over to see her soon. And she definitely wouldn't like kissing. I said to take care, and then I said, 'How's that invalid sister in Coventry doing, by the way?'

She looked blank for a minute, then she said, 'I know you think you're very clever, but I'm not so daft as you make out. I've seen it all. I've been through a war. We had nancy boys in my day, I know about all that. They treat you like you're stupid once you're drawing the pension, but we've lived, and we had better times. All through the blackout and you never heard of a mugging. And there's nothing wrong with Catherine Cookson either. She writes smashing lovely stories with nice people in them, and you can say what you like.'

Catherine Cookson? I never mentioned Catherine Cookson. Well, I did once. About ten years ago I turned down the chance of borrowing one when she offered it to me and the information has obviously been kept on my file.

Yvonne said, 'Take your oranges back, we shan't eat them. I'll phone you. See if you've heard from this Bernard and tell you what they said at the hospital.'

I didn't know anything about a hospital.

'Yeah,' she said, 'didn't I say? I'm sure I said. On the third? I've got to go for an X-ray.'

There was a message on the machine from Eleanor to say St Lucia was dead boring and Nikki was insisting on her wearing lipstick for the wedding. Oh, and happy Christmas, Mum, and thanks for the banana stuff.

I had a long cool shower and suddenly it didn't bother me any more, about being alone on Boxing Day. I decided I'd spend the day in a pair of old leggings and a sweatshirt, clearing out cupboards and making real get-up-and-go lists for the rest of my life. It cheered me up no end knowing that Nikki was scoring patchily in the preliminary rounds of Perfect Stepmother. I was singing 'Glorious Mud' so loudly I didn't hear the phone straight away, and then when I heard it I nearly didn't answer it. I shouldn't have answered it; it was Kim.

She said, 'I know it's a hell of a time to call, but I've been trying to remember how you made those little snacky things out of salami. The ones with the cheese baked on a wafer?'

I said, 'Having a party, Kim? Am I invited?'

She said, 'I'm sorry. Is this a bad time? You must have a houseful.'

I could have told her anything. I could have told her George Hamilton and Imelda Marcos were round playing charades. If Kimberley Kendrick was calling me on some salami and Parmesan wafer-thin pretext, at half past ten on Christmas night, she had to be grovelling, big time.

I said, 'No, I'm on my own. I decided to spend this holiday centring myself. Actually, I was just about to go bed with Raymond Chandler and a Nutella sandwich. Two hundred and thirty degrees for five minutes.'

'Sorry?'

I said, 'The wafers, Kim. Five minutes.'

'Right, thanks. I thought that's what it was.'

'And don't forget the fennel seeds. Have you got fennel seeds?'

She said, 'Yes, I think so. Don't you mind being on your own?'

I said, 'Are you all right?'

Then her voice went thick.

She said, 'We should be friends, Lizzie. Girls like us should stick together. Working in the same jungle. And your bastard left you; mine's left me. It's like . . . sisterhood.'

She'd been on the sauce, no question.

She said, 'I've been on my own all day, Lizzie. All day. Come over and have a drink.'

I told her I'd already had too much to drive, and she started sobbing.

She said, 'I can't stand it. I keep hearing things and there's open fields all round us. I think there's somebody trying to get in . . .'

Wishful thinking, probably.

I said, 'Why don't you take a pill and get some sleep? Things'll look better in the daylight.'

She said, 'I'm not doing pills any more, I'm taking control of my life. Come in the morning; come for the day. You're not doing anything?'

I said, 'Well, I probably am doing something.'

And she cried. 'Oh, please, Lizzie. Please come tomorrow. Please. We can have a really nice day.'

I ummed for a bit longer, but I'd already decided I was going to say yes. I wanted to go to see how much of a mess she was in. People have often turned to me in a crisis, which is great because you get the inside story before anybody else, and sometimes you get extra stuff too, that you can keep to yourself and use in cunning ways.

If there was an errand needed running at Lansdowne Road, or somebody needed sitting with in the sick-room, it was always me they chose. 'Always willing and reliable' it said on my report for second year Juniors, and the bonus was, if there was any excitement, I got the story first. Then I could leak it and have everybody after me, wanting to buy me Trebor chews and hear eye-witness testimony.

119

Like when Janet Coleman had a fit and there was a rumour she'd bitten her tongue off, or when Angela Armitage had to be taken out of the classroom and sent home because her dad had been squashed by a lorry at the brickworks, I was the one asked to sit with them, so I was in possession of the facts.

I called Louie before I set off, to see if I could rope him in, but he wasn't answering. Still down in Cheltenham, I suppose, giving his inheritance prospects a wash and brush up. I pulled yesterday's skirt on, cranberry-sauce stain and all, and a fresh blouse and a spare, in case the ants decided to take another Turkish bath. Then, when I stopped at the Mobil station to get petrol and a box of Quality Street for Kim, it hit me – the whole thing could be a set up. They could be doing me on *This Is Your Life*. It could be just a ruse to get me somewhere, unsuspecting. And maybe Eleanor wasn't in St Lucia at all, and that would explain why Scott kept tittering yesterday. I got so carried away for a minute I dribbled unleaded onto my shoes, and then I pulled over on the forecourt and did my eyes with a kohl pencil in the rear-view mirror, just in case. I didn't want Michael Aspel catching me with my basking-lizard face.

I found the house, no problem. There was a sign made out of a slice of varnished log and Kim's BMW parked on the gravel. She came to the door in a shell suit and puffy eyes. No sign of the man with the big red book;

what a relief. I'd hate to be on *This Is Your Life*. There aren't enough people who know my true qualities to fill a twenty-five minute show. I don't want them doing me until I've got people willing to fly in from California and talk about me with tears in their eyes.

Kim said, 'You look how I feel. I've had a terrible night, I didn't get a wink of sleep.' She was wrong there, I didn't look anything like as rough as she did. I went along with it though. I can play the underdog if that's what people need; I can be very obliging.

She said, 'This is my split-level lounge. You haven't been here before have you?' White carpets, white sofas, chartreuse walls, and glass, glass, glass. Tables, mirrors, little crystal squirrels and bunny rabbits. It must take a whole Filipino to keep everything looking so bright and sparkly.

She said, 'This is my dining room. This is the famous table, I must have told you about this. With the elephant-tusk legs, only they're not real tusks because of Greenpeace and everything. And this is my Murano glass. Everything in this cabinet is Murano.'

We went into the kitchen and she mixed me a drink in a petrol-station tumbler and freshened up her own. She'd got a head start on me with those vodkatinis.

She said, 'This is Bob's room; his Boy's Play Room.'

Leather chairs, wide-screen TV with Nicam stereo, Waverley Novels from Books-by-the-Yard, and a full-size snooker table.

She said, 'I'm not taking him back. If he came all the way from Redditch on his knees, I wouldn't have him back. I do blame her, though; she knew he was married. He brought her here, you know? He actually brought her here.' Sharp intake of breath. When Kim tells you something shocking, she does the gasps of amazement for you. She rushes in with them fast, in case you omit to do them.

She said, 'Girls go mad for him. You've seen him, you wouldn't think he was forty-six, would you? He's still a handsome bastard. You give them the best years of your life . . . And you ruined your body as well; you had kiddies. We never wanted to go in for kiddies. We were the world to one another. And even though he travelled a lot, you know, we were always rock solid. He always brought me something back when he was out in Qatar; he always brought me a little bit of jewellery back from Bahrain. And then this happens. Well, just let him try coming back. I've got rid of all his things: squash racquets, trophies, all his James Herberts.' *Oil Man Finds Library Gutted*.

I told her a few things about Alec. How we were fine through all the years we were trying to have Eleanor and thinking it might not happen, and then when we got her, how he started working late and telling stupid lies that didn't even add up. Sloppy lying's such an insult. In the end I don't think he knew himself if he'd really had a late meeting in Manchester. Everybody thought we made a lovely family, though, even when I was hanging on to the edge of the bed every night for fear of rolling against him and feeling his slippery lying hide.

He told me on a Friday night he was leaving, but he didn't go till Monday morning, so I cooked because I'd already bought a shoulder of lamb, and I did his shirts because I always did them on a Saturday, and he never once looked me in the eye, or carried stuff out to the car, or made phone calls and cut them short when I walked in the room. It was like a murder without any mess. And at the very end I would have had him back if he'd offered, even though the door was wide open and my bright shiny new life, with no football or skid-marked boxer shorts was just waiting to start. I didn't tell Kim that bit, but I did tell her it was Alec's wedding day just dawning over the rim of some palm-fringed bay.

She said, 'We've been to St Lucia. Tobago, Grenada, Antigua, we've been all over. Puerto Rico's always been my favourite though. Shall we have something to eat? You're the expert. I thought you could cook something for us. Just a little snack. Now tell me, honestly, do you think I need to lose weight?'

When a woman has a face like a plate of junket and thighs like barrage balloons honesty isn't what she wants. She wants evasions and somebody else to pity.

I said, 'According to your friend Valerie we all need to. She's always taking a pop at me.'

Kim said, 'She's not my friend. That's just show business. You're my friend.'

123

Oh yeah? That was what Wendy Flitcroft said until Pauline Ogden got a new doll that wet its nappy.

Kim said, 'Have you seen the post bags she gets? The viewers love her. They write in and tell her everything. I think she'll get Woman of the Year. I shouldn't be surprised. People send her presents, you know? To say thank you? And she's getting a rose named after her.'

I said, 'She's a menace. Women were never intended to have flat bellies.'

Kim said, 'I suppose once you've had children you're bound to let things go a bit. I mean, I hardly eat a thing, I just pick at my food. But I do have a very slow metabolism; I was told that by my manicurist. You can tell, apparently, from how slowly the nails grow. Did you see what Valerie gave me? She gave me a leotard from her new collection. I'll show you. I'll fetch it down.'

I was going to have a closer look at her framed photos while she was upstairs, but the vodka had got the better of me. I stayed on the couch, missing Eleanor again. Just a little wave of it breaking over me in the quiet of Kim's lounge. An Eleanor would have made a big difference in Kim's life. All those white carpets. All those posed evening-wear portraits of bastard Bob and wide-eyed Kim.

Then she called me. She said, 'Come up. I haven't finished showing you round. Come and see my babies.'

I took the stairs real slow.

She said, 'Come on in. You'll have to excuse the mess.'

Kim doesn't know the meaning of the word mess. She

knows about flounced bedding and swagged window treatments, and there can't be much she's got left to learn about cuddly toys, but if people want to know about mess, they should come to me.

She was holding up a high-thigh sleeveless leotard in royal-blue nylon and Tactel.

'Look at this,' she said, '*this* goes between the cheeks of your bum. It's a cheese-wire. Try it on. Thirty-nine ninety-nine for a cheese-wire. Go on, try it. Have it, Valerie'll never know. I can lose weight if I want to, I've done it before. Now, this is Marylou. Say hello, Marylou. Hello. And this is Humpty, and this is Mugglewump, and this is Teddy Fat Tum. Say hello, Teddy Fat Tum. Come on, say hello. This is Lizzie. He's sulking. You say hello to him.'

It wouldn't come out.

She said, 'Just say hello. That'll cheer him up.'

''Lo.'

She'd only got basics in the fridge, unless you count Optrex eye masks, and the kitchen floor kept tilting away from me, but I cooked us egg and chips and we were so stuffed we couldn't manage any of the toffee pecan ice-cream till later on. We watched the racing from Haydock and put pretend bets on.

Kim said, 'No, Valerie's very successful, but I don't think she's a very happy person. And she's got super-fluous hair. I don't know if you've noticed. I'd have to get that seen to if it was me. Who shall we talk about now? What do you think of Stuart? Who's the best presenter? If you had to give one of us the chop would you keep me or Stuart? Go on, be honest.'

I'd get rid of both of them. I said, 'Well, you're a team, aren't you? It's hard to picture either of you working with anyone else.' Fortunately her mind had wandered back to Bob, so she didn't notice my shifty answer. I was beginning to see what being Kim's friend might involve.

She said, 'He'll be back. He won't last five minutes in a studio flat. We've got six bedrooms here, you know, all with *en suite*. He'll be back.'

I had a very strong desire to go to sleep.

She said, 'Now what about that Louie? He's a funny boy.'

I said, 'We're friends, me and Louie.'

She said, 'Yes, you always seem very thick. Some women do like that type. Fruit flies, Bob called them. But doesn't it bother you? You know, from a hygiene point of view? That's what'd bother me. Do you let him use your towels?' *Leaking Gays: Laundry Health Scare*.

She said, 'He's quite good, though. His horoscopes are usually pretty good. Has he done your chart for you?'

That was when the vodkatini haze cleared and an extra division of marching ants began sweeping up from the south in a warm wet front to meet the ones fanning out over my neck and shoulders to turn another blouse into a limp rag.

I said, 'Louie doesn't do charts.'

She said, 'He must do. Oh, look at you, are you having a hot flush?'

I said, 'I don't know. Am I? Can we turn the heating down? I've never known him do charts.'

She said, 'Yes, but he could do charts, if somebody asked him.'

I said, 'Well, he did Ancient History at Hull and then he started on the Arts page at the *Yorkshire Post*. I suppose he might have a certificate or something. He might. But I know he started doing it because the usual woman was ill; he was just filling in. And what he does, is, he waits for the monthlies to come out and he pirates them, a bit from one, another bit from somewhere else. He gets all the glossies. Then he passes them on to me when he's finished, good as new, with all the sachets of wrinkle cream still in them. It doesn't matter, none of them mean anything. What are hot flushes like?'

She said, 'Oh, I don't agree. When Jupiter and Pluto were in Libra he said my finances would be getting a boost and I had two wins on the lottery that month. I won a twenty and then a ten. And then he said there might be a confrontation with an Aries, which is my Bob.'

I said, 'Well, he's always told me that Jupiter and Pluto could go retrograde up Uranus for all the difference it'd make. But he knows he makes a lot of people happy, that's why he likes doing it. Course, he'd really like to get on the *Antiques Road Show*, but you can't change tracks so easily once you've done Stars.'

She said, 'Well, I'm sure Meredith thinks he's got certificates. And there's money in Stars. I've done different things. You have to if you want to get to the top. I did *Sunday Praise* for a stint, way back. I did Prestatyn, Filey, Bournemouth, all over. They were recorded, though, and I always think live TV is my strong point. Some people can't hack it, working with an ear-piece, having to think on your feet, but it comes naturally to me. I thrive on it. I shall branch out eventually though: consumer investigations, health, political interviews. Get my own series, doorstepping swindlers and doing campaigns for deprived kiddies. I've got plans.'

I can't see it myself. How can anyone expect to be taken seriously when they've presented *The Midlands This Morning Budget Day Special* wearing Ferragamo mules?

I said, 'Aren't I too young for hot flushes?' and she said, 'Don't ask me. When the day dawns I shall be round to the doctor's for those hormones and I shan't stop them till I fall off my perch. When the day dawns.'

I had to sleep over. We'd been drinking all day, and then I dropped my keys on the gravel anyway and we couldn't find them in the dark, so Kim loaned me a polyester kimono and a Cathay Pacific complimentary wash bag and toothbrush, and I had my pick of five luxuriously appointed guest-rooms.

She said, 'I'm glad you're staying. I hate the nights,' and she kissed me on the cheek.

She's got old lady skin. Blaaaah.

I went out like a light. When I woke, about eight, I lay there for a while with my tongue stuck to the roof of my mouth and counted seventeen different shades of peach, and that didn't include the bathroom. Then the phone rang. Rang and rang, so in the end I thought I'd better pick it up, but my mouth wouldn't work. It was bastard Bob.

He said, 'What took you so long for Chrissakes? Kim? I'll be round later to get the rest of my squash gear. Kim? Are you there? I hope you've not been stupid with your pills again? Kimberley? Kimberley!'

I was out of there. My brain was slamming around against the inside of my skull like a soft-boiled egg, but I was up, out, and dowsing the gravel for my car keys. I needed a shower, a glass of OJ and a few hours under my hollowfibre duvet in a peach-free zone.

Four messages on the machine. Eleanor to say it rained for the wedding. Yvonne to say I left a glove behind. Mum to say it's a pity when you're on the old-age pension and you telephone someone and all you get is a gadget. And Kim to say, 'Heard you leave, but I wasn't decent. Great to meet up with you yesterday, but I'm sure you'll agree, probably best kept between the two of us. Don't want people thinking we weren't out partying, do we? Ciao.'

I made a list.

Put mother on mailing list for stair-lift catalogue.
Never touch vodka again.
Dismantle tree.
Stilton sauce on tagliatelle? Poppy seeds?
Study the collected works of V. Tobin and learn from
her success.

First programme since Christmas this morning and Louie didn't show.

I wanted to go straight round to the flat, but they'd scheduled me between Romanian Orphans and the Health Hazards of Keeping a Dog, so there wasn't time. They replaced Louie with some tape they dragged out about a woman who mends birds' wings on her kitchen table.

Tiff said, 'Meredith's going ballistic. Stuart said no news is good news, but that's not necessarily true because when I was a junior on *Weekend Round-up* we were supposed to have this old guy on, some old pop star, only he didn't arrive and everybody said, "Oh he's famous for it, playing up" and "If he'd been in an accident we'd have heard", and then they broke in and found him electrocuted in his bath. So you never know.'

Cheers, Tiff. That's exactly the kind of story a girl needs to hear when her best friend's missing and she's

131

got to face the cameras in less than fifteen minutes and convey the Fun of Fondue.

It was after twelve before I could get away. I dashed up to see Meredith, but Kim had beaten me to it.

I said, 'Any news?'

He blanked me for a second. He didn't look to me like a man who was pacing the floor, waiting for the phone to ring. The show was in the bag and he was enjoying that 12.05 cigarette.

I said, 'Louie? Any news?'

He said, 'Why? Did you hear something? You going round there now? You got a key?'

I wish. I went round anyway. His blinds were open and everything looked normal. What does normal look like? I stood on the doorstep, wondering if people close the blinds before they hang themselves. Trying to remember if he'd ever told me Strange Cousin Ralph's surname and whether he lived in Chippenham or Chelmsford or Cheltenham.

A car pulled up and a man got out and looked up at the house. He said, 'Any sign? Do you think he's in there?'

This is a thing about me that really gets on my nerves. Anybody else would have said, 'Who are you talking about?' or 'Why are you asking?' but me, I have to pretend I'm in the know and then bluff my way backwards to the facts. It does work sometimes, and you can come out of it looking really cool and smart, but looking cool didn't matter because I just wanted to know where Louie was.

He said, 'Is there a back way in? Have you tried the neighbours?' and he rang all the other bells.

Another car pulled up. A girl with a leather jacket and a tape recorder said, 'Hi, Steve. Anything doing?' She looked through the letter-box and then at me. I should have been away from there, without opening my mouth. Pretended I was a Jehovah's Witness. I should have realized. She said, 'I know you from somewhere, don't I? Are you the *Star?*' and I said, 'No, I'm just a friend.' What a fool. Just a friend. Once she'd wrapped her podgy little fingers round that microphone and stuck it under my nose I'd become *close personal friend and colleague, who is anxious about his state of mind and deeply shocked by the news that he spent last night in the cells, having refused to co-operate with the police and give his name, and appeared this morning at Lozells Magistrates' Court charged under section 32 of the Sexual Offences Act.*

She made a call on her mobile and said, 'No sign of him at his house and his studio aren't commenting till they've talked to him. I've got just under a minute from Lizzie Partridge. She's on the same show. Recent break-up of relationship, but never really talked about his private life, etcetera, but no dirt, so I'm going to go and do the maggot farm protest story and then come back in to edit. But call me if he surfaces.'

She gave me her card and said, 'If you see him, tell him we'd rather get the story from him. Tell him we just want to report the facts.'

Of course, and there goes a squadron of airborne pigs.

Three days and nothing. At least the story's gone off the boil, what with Larry Hagman having liver failure and the Duke of Gloucester visiting Birmingham. Alison phoned me to confirm next week is Rice Made Easy and they hadn't heard anything either. She said, 'Meredith wants to see him soonest, so if you hear from him . . .'

Then, this morning, there was a letter:

Dear heart, Strange Cousin Ralph has kindly availed me of his place at Rustington-on-Sea – a small dank cottage which seems apposite considering the charges brought. No telephone, no electric blanket, and some vino, but oddly no corkscrew, so I'm reduced to talking to myself, wearing my coat in bed and pushing the cork in with a knife. The good news is that SCR had a similar bit of bother years ago, so I'm not disinherited. Also there is a very sweet boy working behind the counter at the chipper where I dine

nightly, incognito. Thank you for my lovely waistcoat, you darling girl. I'm writing to Meredith too,
to tell him when I'll be back. Yours, L.
P.S. At least I can't be accused any more of lacking
conviction.

Sex is such a wrecker. It makes nice people do ridiculous things.

When Mum worked mornings as an egg grader, before
Philip was born, next door used to look after me. Aunty
Jean was quite high up in the kitchens at the infirmary,
but Uncle Dennis was on the social because of his back.
His back always seemed OK to me. We used to listen to
Housewives' Choice, me and Uncle Dennis, and I helped
him with little jobs like polishing Aunty Jean's horse
brasses, or holding the raffia while he tied the chrysan-
themums to sticks. I liked being minded by Uncle Dennis
because they had a cat I could stroke, and we used to
have elevenses which was unheard of in our house. He
had hot milk with Camp coffee essence in it and I had
just hot milk with sugar, and Nice biscuits to dunk, and
the only thing was, sometimes the milk'd get a wrinkly
skin on top. One day Uncle Dennis said I could watch
him take a wiz. I did watch him. I wasn't going to miss
a chance like that. But it wasn't an ordinary wiz he was
taking and he said it was a secret and gave me half a
crown. He quite often gave me a half-crown for our secret
after that, and I had enough for all the *Malory Towers*

books and all the *Famous Fives*, so in a way I suppose you could say some good came out of bad, but Uncle Dennis was never my proper friend after that, and when they moved to Cleethorpes to run a bed and breakfast I never even went out to wave goodbye.

The telephone didn't stop all morning.

First my mother, to say that Mrs Sanderson has been pestering her to sign a petition, and that the Duchess of Kent is unwell after a recent trip to India. She likes the Duchess of Kent.

I said, 'What petition?'

She didn't really know.

'Something about widows' pensions. Something about rights. Everything's *rights* these days.' Sometimes, just occasionally, I do agree with my mother.

She said, 'I'm not signing anything. Look what happened to your Aunty Edie when she signed papers.' *Stupid Woman In Hire Purchase Wrangle*. 'Anyway,' she said, 'I haven't got time for any more rights. Now, I've been tidying, and I want to tell you where the insurance policies are, in case anything happens to me.'

Then Bernard. He sounds promising.

He said, 'Tonya tells me you're a bit of a celebrity in

137

the cookery business. I'm a bit of a celebrity in the pest-control business. You might have heard of us? Ratattack? Not just rats, mind. Fleas, moles, wasps, mice, starling dispersal, pigeon nuisance, woodworm. How about coming out for a drink? How about the Holiday Inn on Wednesday? Half past seven?'

I was still smiling when the phone rang again.

He said, 'You bought my wash boiler.'

I thought, 'Great, he wants it back.'

He said, 'I've got a spin-dryer I'm selling as well. Forty pounds.'

A month ago I was consumed with curiosity about this man. I desired him, I stalked him round the Nip-In.

I said, 'No thank you.'

He said, 'It's a big one. It holds ten pounds.' I told him I had a washer dryer.

He said, 'Well, I thought you should have first refusal. I can deliver.'

I said, 'No thanks. I've got to go, something's burning in the oven.'

I thought of not answering next time it rang, but I wanted it to be Louie.

It was Philip, in such a state. He said, 'They've kept her in. How long do you think they'll keep her in?'

I had to make him go back to the beginning and tell me slowly, and every time I asked him a question he answered something else. I could have done without it. I was starting a cold and I'd got Eleanor slumped over her Creative English homework, deserted by her muse.

I said to Philip, 'So she went for the X-ray?'

'She wasn't allowed anything to eat or drink after midnight.'

'And what happened after that?'

'It wasn't an ordinary X-ray. It was something different.'

'And what happened? You saw the doctor? Afterwards?'

'Yes.'

'And he said . . .?'

'She should stay in. I should come home, pack a bag for her, and she was to stay in.'

'Right. What for? Further tests?'

'Further tests, yes.'

'And what are they testing her for?'

'Just further tests.'

'How long will she be in?'

'Will you visit her?'

I said, 'I can't go tomorrow. I'm doing a Road-Show Cook-In at Worcester and we shan't be back till late. Tell her I'll go on Thursday, if she's still in. She might not be. I'll go Thursday unless I hear she's home. Is she all right though? In herself?'

He said, 'She didn't want to stop in. She was all for coming home and seeing about the tests later, but the doctor said he advised her very strongly not to. That's what he said.'

I said, 'Well, give her my love. And tell her, Thursday.'

He said, 'How long do chops take?'

Eleanor flounced out, fed up with being ignored.

She shouted down the stairs, 'You're always on the phone. You never help me with anything. You're crap. This house is crap. We haven't even got a computer. And you neent think I'm going to college because I'm not.'

Yvonne's got a touch of jaundice. She was propped up in an eau-de-Nil nightie, so much for colour counselling.

She said, 'He's doing everything wrong. He's done Scott's football strip on white cottons, and Kayleigh's jumpers. She's got nothing to wear, and Scott's got a match on Saturday. Would you have time to take him? Can you take him after school? It's no use asking Phil. He don't know if he's coming or going, and the cheque book's in my name. I could sign him a cheque for cash, but you know what he's like. He'll get the wrong thing. I dread to think what I'm going back to. He mixes all the cloths up. Everything ends up a floor cloth — tea towels, everything. I shall have to chuck them all out and start again. You have to depend on people for every mortal thing when you're in here. If they don't send me home soon I shall just have to walk out. They don't realize, these doctors; they've all got Swedish au pairs. They don't realize, when you've got a family you can't lie around

141

slacking. My nets haven't even been done. I always wash my nets after New Year.'

Good old Yvonne. No watching the clock, wondering what to talk about next, when you visit her in hospital. Just take a notepad and write down your orders; that's what she needs. Directing ops from Ward G5.

I felt weird after I left her. I'd never seen her in bed before and it didn't seem right. Even when she'd had Kayleigh and Scott she was up and about straight after, wiping disinfectant over everything, waking them up for their next feed so they didn't mess up the timetable and put her behind with her ironing.

I went down to the coffee-shop and bought a cup of tea. I thought I'd just sit for a while, think things over, and write down what I had to do before I forgot:

Eleanor's old jumpers for Kayleigh?
Tell Philip to get a cheque book and grow up.
Check he's OK for food.
Wash net curtains VERY CAREFULLY.
Take Scott shopping.
Volunteer to be boiled in oil instead.

A man came and sat at my table, coffee slopped into his saucer.

He said, 'I hope you won't mind my saying that I use your recipe for beef cooked in beer all the time, and I think your marmalade ice-cream is out of this world.'

It was only the second time anyone had come up to me like that, and the first time it was a woman who wanted me to get her Stuart's and Kim's autographs.

I said, 'Oh. Oh, yes. Well, thank you very much,' or it might have been, 'Much, yes, you thank, oh, oh.' I need more practice.

He said, 'You must get tired of people coming up to you like this. I just wanted you to know you've got a fan.'

I started to get back my power of coherent speech.

I said, 'No, I'm pleased you did. It's nice to know someone's out there watching.'

He said, 'Never miss it. I took early retirement to look after my wife. Daytime TV's been a good pal to me. Are you here visiting?'

I told him. He said, 'Have half of my Danish pastry. You look starved. Which ward is she on?'

He was a man who knew his way round. He said, 'G5. That's women's surgical. My wife was in there once, but she's on D2 now – oncology. That's cancer. She's in for them to try some new injections, but there's not very much more they can do for her. She's in a pretty bad way.'

I said the things you say. A woman from the WRVS came and wiped the table round us.

He said, 'I feel a bit of a fraud when people start offering me their condolences. Fact is, if she hadn't got ill we'd have gone our separate ways by now, but as things have worked out, the cancer's going to finish it for us. She's been in and out of here for nearly two years now. She's had a rough passage. And I shall end up the widower who nursed his wife instead of the husband who ran off, so I shall come out of it smelling of roses. Funny how things turn out.'

I said, 'Does she know?'

He said, 'About dying, yes. About how close I came to leaving her, not officially, but she's not stupid. We both sort of decided on this without talking about it. It wouldn't be what I wanted if it was me that was ill, would it you? Dragging things out with somebody you don't even like any more?'

I said, 'Is that what they call a dilemma?'

He said, 'I think it is. Have you got a family?'

I gave him the abridged version because they were pulling the shutters down at the counter and the volunteer ladies had got their coats on. He was going back up to D2.

He said, 'What have you got lined up for us next week?' So I told him about the risotto, buttery and creamy with Parmesan flaked on the top.

He said, 'Grand. I can't wait. Tom, by the way. Tom Sullivan. It's been a real thrill to meet you, and I hope your sister-in-law's soon on the mend.'

What a lovely man. Nudging a size sixteen and he thought I looked starved.

I picked up Scott outside the school gate, mud all over his trousers and his Nike Air Maxes. He got into the car like he was climbing naked into a tumbril on his way to be tarred and feathered. I asked him what he'd been doing.

'Nuffing.'

I said, 'Yeah. Eleanor seems to do a lot of that. What's your teacher's name?'

'Mr Sutton.'

I said, 'Does he read you stories?'

'Can't remember.'

'What about projects? Don't you do projects with him?'

'Canals.'

I said, 'That's a good one. Have you been to Gas Street Basin?'

'Millions of times.'

'And have you done about Venice? Have you seen pictures of Venice?'

He thought it was a trick question. He looked at me hard, trying to work out the answer, just like his dad.

I said, 'In Venice they have canals instead of roads and streets. Everything has to be brought in on boats. Milk, baked beans, fish fingers, settees, football gear. It all comes on boats. Has to.'

'CD-ROMs?'

'Yes.'

'Comics?'

'Yep.'

He said, 'Yeah, I knew that,' and I could see I'd got a little bit of a fingerhold on that mind of his, worn shiny by the telly.

I said, 'Well, if you lived in Venice instead of Perry Barr, you'd have to get a boat to go to school, and your dad'd have to get a boat to go to the Leccy Board. And then, say you needed your window mending or something, the workman'd have to come by boat, and when somebody dies, even the coffin has to be brought in on a boat. And hundreds of years ago, if somebody did something bad and they got the death sentence, they'd tie weights to his legs and row him out to one of the big canals at night and throw him overboard, then leave him to drown.'

Interested silence. Got him.

He said, 'You drive slower than my mum. Anyway, if they did that to me I'd quickly get the weights off and swim home.'

146

I said, 'You'd have your hands tied behind your back.'

'Well,' he said, 'I'd swim back anyway because I'm a good swimmer. I'd swim like this . . .'

And while I tried to reverse into a tight space in the multi-storey, he did a sea-lion impersonation.

'. . . and then I'd cut the ropes on something sharp and put a disguise on and get a laserblaster and I'd go round to the prison and atomize everybody, nya-a-a-a-a-a-a . . .' He kept the laserblaster rattle going all the way round to City Sports.

I told the woman she'd have to measure him because he was my nephew and I didn't know his size. I wanted her to know right from the start that that little no-neck wasn't mine.

She said, 'You're a lucky lad. I wish I had an aunty to take me shopping. And who's your team?'

'Year Five.'

'What colour do they wear?'

'Yellow and black.'

'And who do you support?'

'Villa.'

'And what's their colours?'

'Clariot and blue.'

'That's right. Good lad. Yellow and black, chest twenty-eight. There you are. Do you need the socks?'

We bought it all. The full nine yards. Then I took him for a burger.

He said, 'That place? Where do they play football?'

I told him there were some little squares where you could kick a ball about. I said I didn't think they played a lot of football in Venice.

'Rubbish place,' he said.

When I dropped him off, Kayleigh said Philip was at the hospital and Yvonne was probably coming home tomorrow. She didn't want any of Eleanor's jumpers. She said she was getting everything new.

I said, 'See you then, Scott.'

He didn't say goodbye or thank you, just did his impersonation of a judicial drownee undulating through the water in a daring bid to cheat death.

I bought a pink jacket and a navy skirt for meeting Bernard and had a wash and blow-dry. I looked really great. Cornelian earrings, big black coat and a good long squiff of Anais Anais. Then suddenly I lost it. This happens sometimes when I'm looking great. I only don't get nervous when I'm wearing my old mac and no eye-shadow. I was there too early as well, and I didn't want to read a paper because of the newsprint rubbing off, so I sat reading the metric conversion tables in the back of my diary.

We had a drink and then Bernard said, 'How about a spin out to The Olde House At Home for a steak?' He's a seedy-looking guy. Hair receding a bit. Vulpine. I quite like that. His Mercedes was parked under the hotel. He said, 'What do you drive?' He roared when I told him.

He said, 'Famous TV star like you. I should have thought you'd have a nice little Golf convertible. I love my car. When I'm out with a lady I like to know I'm sitting on some serious throttle. You know?'

We had steak Béarnaise and a cuddle in the Merc before he dropped me off, which overstepped Tonya's first-date rules by a mile, but Bernard had been making it clear all evening how attractive he found me and I wasn't going to let that go off the boil. I'd forgotten how good a man can smell. And he's nice. He asked me about the show and the studio, and whether we ever have any trouble with cockroaches. And he doesn't mind spending his money – he insisted on getting me a Bisquit Dubouche instead of an ordinary brandy. He drives a bit fast, but then, I've always been nervous about speed. We travelled by Midland Red Bus when I was a kid and they'd no sooner peaked at 27 m.p.h. than it was time to slow down for the next stop.

Mum and Dad did get a car eventually, but it was after I'd left home. They got a three-wheeler with fibreglass bodywork because Mum said Dad was too old to go taking driving tests. That was when they started having holidays. Crawling up the middle of mountain roads with half of Wales's tourist trade stuck behind them, trying to get past, and Mum saying, 'Ignore them, Wilf. We've got every right.' That's where road rage was born. Aberglaslyn 1968.

So Bernard likes to put his foot down. I tried not to be too obvious about gripping the edge of my seat and braking; I tried to laugh gaily, except when he was being serious, of course. It's amazing how a nice guy like that could have had such a bitch of a wife. I'm seeing him again at the weekend.

Louie's back. He phoned me first and said, 'Expect an old friend to walk back into your life. And as Saturn moves away from the romance area of your life, prepare for exciting relationship changes.'

I said, 'Everything sorted?'

He said, 'Pretty much. I haven't got a date for the hearing yet. I'm going in tomorrow to see Meredith and get my botty smacked, but I think I might get a raise as well. I should do, they got loads of letters, did they tell you? From viewers. It worked out that seventy-five per cent thought I should be given a job for life and made a Knight of the Garter, and the rest wanted my *cojones* cut off and stuffed in my mouth, preferably live on TV. Which reminds me, Chas got in touch. See what happens when you hit the headlines?'

It was so good to see him. He thinks Chas might be angling to get back with him and I hope it happens because Chas is steady, and they'd be like a proper married couple instead of Louie hanging round toilets and turning up strangled one of these days.

I was doing Winter Soups between Quit Smoking With Acupuncture and How to Wear the New Skirt Length, but I got squeezed up a bit because they let the phone-in on Will Charles Ever Be King? run over time. I did French Onion, Italian Bean and Broccoli with Stilton. Louie tasted them all and he said, 'I'm not much of a soup person myself, but I'll tell you what I do like: tinned tomato. Heinz.' So I went back to his flat after the show and that's what we had.

I told him about Bernard. He said, 'Hm.' I hate it when he does that. And what does he know? I said to him, 'What do you know? You never keep anybody for five minutes and you're always getting roughed up or ripped off.'

He said, 'Goes with the territory, heart. Testosterone territory,' and he laughed, but I still wished I hadn't said it.

I told him about Kim and Boxing Day and Teddy Fat Tum, and how she doesn't seem to want to be my sister in adversity any more. I said, 'She's such a flake. Talking about doing political stuff and she's got her bed covered with gonks.'

He said, 'Well, I rather like her, in a light blue touch paper and retire kind of way. I think she's got balls. I can imagine her getting her eye bags done and wearing a Norma Desmond turban and just going on and on for years.'

I went to the Nip-In on the way home to get something for Eleanor's tea and there was a really gorgeous young blade in there buying a snack you can eat between meals without ruining your appetite, couldn't take his eyes off me. I thought, 'This is the buttered-bun phenomenon. One kiss from Bernard has turned me into an object of desire.'

I was cool. I just stared back and took my time. I wanted to be sure he'd remember me the next time we met. I didn't know about the tomato-soup stain all round my mouth until I looked in a mirror at home.

Yvonne's home. She said they'd found a little blockage and done a little op to clear it and she's to go back in four weeks for a check-up.

I said, 'You should take things easy. Rest up a bit. I'll come over when I can.'

'No,' she said, 'I'm right as ninepence. I feel better when I'm on the go. You'll have to bring this Bernard round so we can have a look at him.'

We're not quite at that stage yet, me and Bernard. We're still at the steak-dinner-and-front-seat-fumble stage, but tonight . . . Tonight we're seeing the new de Niro movie at the multi-screen near his place, so we could well be talking nightcaps followed by matters arising.

Louie's been nagging me again about my career. Meredith seems to have decided that that little brush with the law has made him hot stuff, so he can do no wrong at the moment. He keeps saying, 'Books, videos, heart. Let's get cracking. Let's clean up.' And I was going to start work this afternoon on my brilliant future. Write down some ideas to make Hegarty see pound signs and shift his idle carcass, but I can always do that tomorrow. You only get one chance to make a first impression with your peachy perfect thighs.

To Do:

Cuticles.
Cold tea bags on eyes. Listerine.
Bosom-contouring gel.
Dry hair with head upside down for extra volume.
Be spontaneous.

Tiffs pregnant. I'd guessed before she told us; I'd know that blotchy tired-out look anywhere. She was riding high, though, giving everyone a molecule-by-molecule progress report.

She said, 'Well, we've actually known for a couple of weeks, but I've been having a few cramps and my mum lost three that way, out shopping and she started haemorrhaging, so we thought best to keep it under our hats until we're out of the woods, although, I mean everything else is normal, I've been sick every morning and Neil says he can see a difference in my boobs already, so it looks like being plain sailing . . .'

Louie put his fingers in his ears. He said, 'Stop it, it's horrid. I don't want to hear another cliché.'

Tiff said, 'What? Oh, you men. Neil was the same. If ever I had a tummy ache or anything, you know, women's things, he'd say, "I don't want to know about that," but now he's really into it. He's been looking round to see if he can get a little Babygro suit in Villa's colours. Anyway, Louie, I don't want you going all peculiar on me. When it's born, I want you to do its stars. It's going to be a Virgo so I want to know what colours to do the nursery and everything. And when we've had that test, we shall know if it's going to be a little boy or a little girl, only I don't know if I want to know before it's born, and Neil says he knows it's a boy anyway, so, and something I've gone right off is coffee. I can't bear it; not even the smell of it. And that was actually how I knew first of all, because Neil's mum made me a cup and I thought, Well, I don't fancy this. I suppose it's your body's way, you know? Because they say caffeine's bad for the unborn child, don't they, only there's supposed to be more caffeine in tea than coffee and I do still enjoy my cuppa. And I've stopped drinking because that's bad for you, and we're going to read all the books and go to all the classes, because when you think about it, it's a brand-new little life and you want everything to be perfect . . .'

There was no sign of Tiff stopping to draw breath so I went for a wander, to see whether Omar Sharif had arrived.

Stuart said Kim was with him, going through the questions. He said, 'Amazing coincidence, Tiffany comes in with her lovely news and I've got a bit of an announcement to make myself. We've got another one on the way – October. It's a bit sooner than we'd planned, but as Dawn says, we may as well get it all over and done with.'

157

Well, well. Last time I was trapped in the lift with Stuart, he told me Dawn thought full-time motherhood was a time of magic and joy and jolly farmyard mobiles; now it's something to get over and done with. I guess this means the Infant King is walking. Stuart's pregnant, Tiffs pregnant. So according to the Clarke Family Rule of Three I must be about to hear of a third pregnancy. Good things, bad things, births, deaths, they all travel around in trios. It was my mother who propounded this theory, but if you live with silly talk when you're at an impressionable age, some of it is bound to rub off on you. March 1957, say, I passed for the grammar school, Dad won seventeen shillings on a Vernon's treble chance, and a coal lorry ran out of control on the Harborough Road and nobody was hurt. August 1959, Philip knocked the spout off the good teapot, Mum lost her purse on the bus and never got it back even though her address was in it, and Uncle Cyril got a double hernia. November 1963, our rabbit, Bugsie, Dad's foreman at the brick-works, and President John F. Kennedy all passed over. And the summer of 1964, two women my mum knew from the biscuit factory had baby boys and so did the Queen. And then there's the Holy Trinity.

When I went back in to get my hair combed through Tiff was in full flood about epidurals and Louie was looking pretty sick.

He said, 'I can't cope with another six months; all this talk about dark pulsating tissues. And how come you're

158

looking so peaky? Bernie the Exterminator not treating you right?'

I was all ready to tell him when Tobin walked in, in a draped, cream, jersey trouser suit and a tight black belt. 'Ooh,' he said, only not quietly enough, 'it's the Food Gestapo. Hide your Creme Eggs.'

She said, 'You may as well hear this from me. I've just come from Meredith and I've told him, either he gets his schedules sorted out or I leave. They've got no business letting you do these awful suet pudding things the same morning I'm on. I've told him, you'll have to do something appropriate like low-fat dips, if you're capable, which I doubt. I mean, it's me they switch on for, after all. Today's woman doesn't want to know about treacle sponge.'

Louie said, 'Today's man does.'

She said, 'I'll come back later, Tiffany. There's a nasty smell in here at the moment.'

Louie squeezed my hand. He said, 'Never mind about her. We don't like her do we? Tell me about Bernie. Did he take you back to the ranch? Has he got squirrel heads mounted on wall plaques? Or killer bees?'

The thing with Louie is, you can give him the unvarnished truth. Whatever you've done, whatever shitty little incident has occurred, he could probably top it if he wanted to. So I told him how we were on our way back from the movie when Bernard asked if I'd like to see his business premises, and how I finished up in the back of

159

a Ratattack van (Ministry of Agriculture and Fish approved, unmarked vehicles on request) with Bernard on top of me, in far too much of a hurry to savour my perfumed skin and oyster silk camisole.

Louie said, 'Well, sometimes impetuosity can be exciting.'

'It wasn't.'

'Or flattering?'

I said, 'My tights got laddered. My jacket got stuff on it – cockroach stuff. And Bernard lasted about ten seconds.'

Louie said, 'The beast. Are you hurt?'

I told him I wasn't. Not that kind of hurt.

He said, 'I hope you didn't leave him in any doubt. I hope you told him to be gone from your life and to never more darken your door? Heart? Speak to me. Tell me you're not giving him one last chance? Elizabeth! What am I going to do with you? Someone should go round and sort out these Bernards and Terences and Kevins. I'd do it myself if I didn't get asthma. Ask Tiff about the jacket though; she's very gifted with stains. And I'll see you later, I promise. I'll take you for a hot chocolate with extra whipped cream. But I must just say hello to Omar and tell him how much I loved him in *Dr Zhivago*.'

I've never dated anyone called Kevin.

Kim was all pumped up after the celebrity interview, wriggling around with her skirt above sea level, licking the spoon from my lemon-curd pudding. Then she got testy. Stuart was doing the piece on the campaign to make pubs more child-friendly, which he said was a super smashing idea. Kim said, 'I don't agree. If I go into a pub the last thing I want is children grizzling and knocking their pop over.'

Stuart said, 'But then you're discriminating against people with children. It's hard enough in this country; we're so anti-children, parents are made to feel like nuisances.'

Kim said, 'Well, a lot of them are. They take their kids out and let them run wild, wandering round restaurants, clambering up the back of the banquettes. Just because you choose to have children, that's no reason I should have to put up with them when I've gone out for a quiet drink.'

Stuart said, 'It's a good job some of us do *choose* to have children, because those children that you find so offensive when you're out wining and dining, some of them are going to be the doctors and nurses you'll be glad to have looking after you when you're old and in your wheelchair. That's what I say to people who complain about little children.'

The Licensed Victualler's spokesman's eyeballs were going back and forth like Chinese ping-pong balls.

Kim said, 'Pubs are for grown-ups, Stuart. And nobody *has* to go to the pub; it's not like the supermarket. And what I think is, if you choose to have children, you should do your drinking at home, or pay for a babysitter. Time for a break. Stay with us for Valerie Tobin's brand-new action plan to help you Rediscover That Waist.' She did wait till we were off air before she gave Stuart the finger. *Sexual Chemistry Failure: TV Bosses Quizzed*.

Louie had been watching her on the monitor. He punched the air and said, 'Go, my proud beauty, go! And tell him his jumpers smell of ickypoo.'

Sometimes I think he likes Kim more than he likes me.

Bernard's one of those guys who thinks when a woman says no she means maybe. He's phoned me every day since that tender sharing moment round the back of Hagley Industrial Park, trying to fix up our next date, even though I told him I wouldn't have a free evening for years.

He said, 'Is it my line of business? That's it, isn't it? There was another lady I was seeing at one time. She got very upset about badgers.'

I said, 'No, it's not the business. It's the van,' which was only a fraction of the truth. 'I'm getting too old for sex in the back of a van.'

'Course you're not,' he said. 'Age is all in the mind.'

I couldn't come right out with it. Thou Shalt Not Cause Upset was the first commandment in our house and early training stains deep.

You learn to store things up and smile, and just say the things you should have said quietly to yourself. You

163

let people push in front of you in the line for school dinners, and slide manky apples into your bag from the back of the stall, and you smile and plan how you'll get your own back some day, when it's more convenient. But sometimes little bits seep out; things you should have shouted about in 1954, say. And the bits that leak out are boiling hot and putrid. You say you're mad because you've been waiting all morning for the plumber, but actually it's because you've been waiting forty years to cause an upset and you still haven't really got what it takes to do it.

He said, 'Come on, how about a nice spin out? How about a run out to the Bygones Theme Park and then on to the Cannock for a slap-up dinner? Say you'll think about it, at any rate?'

I said I'd think about it. I'm not going to though.

The next thing was, I was trying to thread a needle, to stitch the button back onto the raincoat I like because I've been wearing the raincoat I don't like all week, and I couldn't see to do it, didn't matter which way I turned the lamp, and my heart started puttering, fast, then missing a beat, then fast again, and I thought, If those ants start up now I'm going to scream, and they did, so I did. I screamed and screamed and pulled my jumper off before the sweats ruined it, and threw the sewing tin at the wall, and then I began to feel better, even though it boomeranged and chipped a glass Eleanor had left for the maid to clear away, and I'm going to be finding buttons

164

and pins in that corner for all eternity. I went upstairs and looked at my reflection, without putting the bathroom light on. I saw somebody who looked just like my mother in 1962, except for the grey satin teddy and the cheap earrings. I made the ugliest faces I could at her, and she made them back at me, and after that I floated to bed and fell into a deep and wonderful sleep.

Tonya said, 'Well, dear, you've made a big hit with Bernard.'

I know, but I'm not going to see him again, and it's not easy to tell that to a man who's bought three dinners and a movie. It's got to be done though. I read this article called 'Ten Steps to Self-Assertiveness' while I was waiting to get my teeth descaled. And one of the things about Bernard is, he doesn't pick up hints. He's like a puppy who's piddled on your carpet and eaten all your shoes; he still thinks you'll be really pleased to see him. The phone rings and it's Bernard again, ready to let you throw his stick.

I said, 'Tonya, it's not working for me. You're going to have to tell him. I have tried, but he won't take no for an answer.'

She said, 'What do you mean?'

I said, 'I'm not going into details. Just tell him to stop calling me.'

She said, 'Well, I'm very disappointed to hear this. You've been my star couple this month. Maybe you need to give it a bit more time? Maybe you're expecting too much too soon?'

I told her. I said, 'I've got bruises, Tonya. Is that what you'd call too much too soon?'

She said, 'Now look here. My gentlemen know how to behave. Are you making allegations?'

I said, 'Yes, and I'm cancelling. Take me off your books.'

She said, 'Well, this is hardly a helpful attitude. I'm afraid I always had some doubts about your attitude. You see, I question whether you ever really wanted to meet new people. Attitude is everything.'

I said, 'Oh, I thought a manicure and a Wonderbra were everything.' She just sighed. Then she said, 'You do realize there can be no question of a refund?'

I said, 'Just wipe my file. Put me through your paper shredder. And by the way, you'll be interested to hear, the thing that drove Bernard wild with lust was my forty-four inch hips, so stick that up your parson's nose, if there's room up there after you've shoved my special-offer non-refundable six-month membership.' OK, those might not have been my exact words, but she definitely caught me on one of these bad-tempered power surges I've started getting, and afterwards I felt great. I cut myself a big doorstep of panettone and dunked it in a deep steaming bowl of cappuccino.

Eleanor's been in a strange mood since she got back. She's hardly mentioned the wedding. I did hear her on the phone telling my mother how Nikki had to get married in calamine because of a heat rash and how they had to queue for the bridal arbour because there were five other weddings booked for the same afternoon. The only bit she'd told me about was Alec getting called by his office and told to get back pronto and Nikki crying about it. She said, 'Dad told Nikki she could stay on without him but she wouldn't. I would of.'

'Have.'

'Wha'?'

'You would *have*.'

'God!'

Romantic as ever, Alec. 'Gotta get back, sweetie. People to see, papers to sign. You stay.' I wonder whether Nikki's had a birthday with him yet. 'Get yourself something, sweetie. Pick something out and charge it. I never know what to get.'

Anyway, Eleanor's been glum and spotty since she got back, and Gavin's stopped coming round. It could just be that. And she's got exams next term; she could be worrying about those. I don't think she is though. When I came off the phone from Tonya I found her in front of the fire filling in *The Play and Learn Book of Dot-to-Dot Dinosaurs*. I'm sure she's meant to be revising *Twelfth Night*.

I said, 'You all right, Elly?'

Unsolicited enquiry. Invasion of privacy. Patronizing use of baby name. Squirm. Shrug.

I said, 'No Gavin?'

'Chucked him.'

Caution. Narrow conversational opening. Reduce chumminess NOW.

I said, 'Sorry, didn't realize. Was he shitty about your going away at Christmas?'

'Just chucked him, that's all.'

Major taboo ahead. Stop. Think. Engage brain before opening mouth.

'Yes,' I said, 'sometimes it has to be done. I chucked Bernard.'

Uh-oh. A girl doesn't want to hear that kind of talk from her mother. She concentrated even harder on her stegosaurus, and dived for the telephone on its first half ring.

'Yeah,' she said. 'What? Really? Ah, great. When?

Brilliant? Yeah? Ah, triffic. Yeah. OK. It's Dad,' she said. 'He wants to talk to you.'

'This bill,' he said, 'for contact lenses? Are you out of your fucking mind?'

I said, 'You told her she could have them. You told her to get them.'

He said, 'I never said she could definitely have them. Nikki said they might look nice for the photos, but I never told her to go ahead and get them. I'm not paying, Lizzie. We've gotta talk about money anyway, you're gonna have to take a cut. I can't be expected to keep paying you the full whack and pay for her to come to Boston and look after her while she's here. You know? And it's not as though you're not doing all right. I mean, you must be doing OK. And, I mean, you got your usual money in December and she was out there with us for ten days. And times are tough, you know? The recovery's slow in coming. Everybody's downsizing and that's what we gotta do too.'

I said, 'Alec, either you keep sending the money as agreed or I send you Eleanor. Do you want it in writing from my solicitor? You don't have a clue what she costs me. I only have to ask her to rinse a few cups and it costs me a transatlantic phonecall. So just don't try it on, Alec. You're not hard up. Anyway, what have you told her that's cheered her up so much?'

'Ask her,' he said and slammed the phone down.

She was in the kitchen, fridge door open, just looking.

'Dad and Nikki are having a baby,' she said. 'Wicked.'

Downsizing. Of course.

She said, 'I'm going to go and stay and help with the baby.'

I tried to look serene and unaffected, and say things about having to fit around exam schedules and babies not always arriving exactly when they're supposed to, without dampening her happiness. I waited till she'd gone up to her room before I really allowed myself to think about Alec and Nikki starting a whole new life together in a whole new country, with a little baby and Eleanor there with them as mother's help and proud half-sister, sleeping till afternoon and running up the phone bill and leaving the freezer door open and wrecking their state-of-the-art Italian coffee machine. Then I danced. I moved the chairs, kicked back the rug and I danced, with a song in my heart and another wedge of panettone in my hand.

Kim and Stuart are off the show for three weeks. Officially they're on holiday and we've got Cliff and Janey Lassiter the hot young media marrieds filling in. I heard Kim was booked in somewhere like the Belvedere for a five-star detox, but her driver told Tiff he took her to Heathrow to catch a flight to San Francisco.

I don't see her coming back. I think she's finished. Seeing how Janey and Cliff keep things rattling along, making little jokes, touching thighs, I'd say Kim and Stuart will be getting their P60s, any minute now.

The other thing is, Meredith – he's being very attentive. He was knocked out by my date and toffee pudding and he came down specially to compliment me on my stir-fries. He said it couldn't have been easy going on straight after Inside the Mind of a Serial Killer, and I'd struck exactly the right note. Now he keeps looking at me. He waves when he passes me in the car park; he never used to wave. It's crazy, but after all this time I think Meredith's taken a fancy to me. It can happen. And that's exactly the kind of helping hand my career could do with. Who knows, a little pillow talk and Turtle Face Tobin could be history too.

Yvonne's getting up a crowd to go and see the Hunkies. They're doing two shows at the Apollo and if she can fill three more seats she gets one free.

She said, 'What about Eleanor? Little Maureen's girl's coming; she's about Elly's age. And you must know somebody else you can ask. It's a really good night out.'

I said, 'Where would we be sitting? I'm not coming if we're going to be at the front.'

I've heard about these shows. They come down into the audience wearing nothing but posing pouches, and I'm not ready to die yet, slowly, of embarrassment, in front of a crowd of thousands.

She said, 'The front's all booked up. These will be too if we don't get a move on. I need to know tomorrow night latest, so don't let me down. You can have a photo taken afterwards; it's like a personal souvenir. Kayleigh's dared me, so I'm going to get one done. Get our Phil to buck up his ideas a bit.'

I said, 'But what do they do? Do they take everything off?'

She said, 'Well, they do and they don't. They don't do anything really mucky, not like the one they hired for Karen's hen night. He did audience participation in Rita's dinette for twenty pounds extra.'

I said, 'And what did he do?' but she said, 'Ask Rita.'

Seventeen quid to see men with streaked hair not doing anything really mucky. Is that good value? Actually, it's not the money; it's being there with Rita and the two Annes and all Yvonne's usual crowd, having to pretend that watching a man with a pink balloon in front of his willy is a riot.

I was trying to explain it to Louie. I said, 'You know I'm not a prude. You know I'm not stuck-up.'

'No,' he said, 'you don't *mean* to be stuck-up, but heart, we both know you prefer being on the outside, looking in, letting everybody else make idiots of themselves. And you can't chop and change; you can't be one of the gang all of a sudden. See, I don't really count because you're not like that with me, but I do know what you're like, holding back, getting stuff on people, sneering in the shadows. You know you said to me no one ever stops you in the street? How no one ever recognizes you, even though you're on the programme nearly every week and sometimes your picture's in the *TV Times?* That's why. It's because you're never really there, so nobody ever really sees you. You're the invisible sneerer. Don't look

175

at me like that; I'm your friend. I can tell you things. Now, the Hunkies. Will your Yvonne allow men? If she will, put me down for two tickets. It's time I lowered the tone of Chas's life again.'

So that's that. Louie and Chas are definitely back together and I'm a sneerer, and invisible. That's all he knows. I'm glad I didn't say anything about Meredith. He's still smiling at me enigmatically, but that can be my little secret.

I told Louie I'd have to check with Yvonne because I thought it was going to be strictly a girls' night out, but Yvonne was all for it.

'Course he can come,' she said. 'Big Rita'll go mad. She'd like to take him home and keep him.'

I said, 'You'd better not tell Philip. He won't like it if he knows they're coming. All those names he calls them.'

'No,' she said, 'it wouldn't bother him. As long as he doesn't meet one of them down a dark alley. Live and let live, but just keep your back to the wall, that's what he says. Anyway, he's got an old motor bike in pieces on the garage floor, so he's not interested in what I'm up to. Has your mum phoned you about her blackouts? Apparently she came over giddy pegging her washing out and then she had a funny turn in Pricerite and they had to fetch her a chair and a glass of water. So she's back under the doctor. I might drive up on Sunday and see if she's all right.'

Eleanor blew her bubble gum so big that when it collapsed she had to pick it off her cheeks. She said, 'When am I going to stay with Dad and Nikki?' Which was the damnedest question because there was a letter for her from Boston this morning, and I'd steamed it open in case there was a cheque in it for me. There wasn't, just the news that Nikki, poor thing, is having the most horrendous complications, rare blood group, family history of twins, and the whole thing is terribly tricky, plus, Daddy had just lost a really major client and there have been so many things to get for the new house, so funds are a bit low right now, button, which makes half-term out of the question and frankly Easter looks difficult, but definitely in the summer?

He has no idea. I know Eleanor; she'll have told everyone in school about going to the States every holiday and getting a baby brother or sister. All that business about having her own room decorated how she wants it and how easy it'll be, using his Air Miles to fly her over, and what a little jet-setter she'll get to be. He's forgotten he ever said any of it.

I said, 'I don't know yet. I expect they're busy settling in.' I'll buy a glue-stick in the morning and reseal her letter, and I'll buy some corn for her to pop too, and rent an Eddie Murphy movie. In a way this could be just what we need to bring us closer together.

So much for Louie being *my* friend. Big Rita monopolized him all evening. He was right down at the farthest end of the row, Yvonne one side of him, Rita the other, pink and chortling and playing the celebrity queer.

I was between Little Maureen and Chas. He looked as comfortable as a vicar at a rave.

I said, 'What are we doing here?' and he said, 'Anything to keep him happy. That's what *I'm* doing here. I'd sooner see *Les Miserables On Ice*. That's how much I want to be here.'

I said, 'Are you properly back together then? Is it for keeps?'

He said, 'Well, don't bank on a silver anniversary or anything, but it's as for keeps as anything ever is with Louie.'

Little Maureen started stamping and shouting 'Gerramoff,' as soon as the lights went down. Boys with big salon-tanned shoulders, bumping and grinding to

'Leader of the Pack.' Chas paid solemn attention; he could have been at a Reith Lecture. I just smiled. I faked it to start with, but then when the Hunkies went down into the front stalls with their bottles of baby oil, I really smiled, because we were in the circle, in the middle of a row. We were safe.

They were all going for photographs afterwards and then for pizza, except Louie, because Chas didn't want him to, and Yvonne. She says the tablets they've put her on make her tired.

Louie said, 'Well, if I'm not allowed a souvenir photo are we coming back to your house for lovely things to eat?' So I went on ahead and made a quick hollandaise while Chas and Louie fetched two bottles of Australian fizz from their fridge, and we had a late late supper of eggs Benedict and crisp maple-smoked bacon.

Louie said, 'Where's the teen she-devil?'

I said, 'She's sleeping over at Emma's or Gemma's,' but she wasn't. Later on, when we'd been making a lot of noise for grown-ups and Louie had done the Dance of the Seven J Cloths, Chas went into the bathroom and found her on the floor, overdosed on Menoplus, the perfect one-a-day nutritional supplement for women in the middle years, and alcoholic lemonade. She'd read Alec's letter.

Chas offered to stay and help, but there was nothing much we could do and Louie had his coat on, keen to leave before there was any vomiting.

I tucked her in with her polar-bear pyjama case. I hadn't been in her bedroom in a very long time. I used to read to her every night and play snakes and ladders and try not to let her see me looking at my watch because we were supposed to be having Quality Time. I used to change her sheets, and buy her new PJs, and open her window to let the smell of the honeysuckle drift in. I suppose she changes her own sheets now. She's got magazine pages all over her walls: photos of boys with moody eyes and their flies unzipped. She has still got some of her little dollywhat's-its on her shelves, like her Pound Puppy and the knitted tiger Alec's mother made for her, but she's certainly past the stage of reading *Bunty*.

I said, 'You all right? You didn't take anything else?'

'No,' she said, 'I didn't know where you were. Where were you?'

I told her. I said, 'You should have seen Aunty Yvonne. I never knew she could whistle with two fingers in her mouth. Was it just Dad's letter that upset you?'

'Yeah,' she said. 'He said I could go every school holiday if I wanted to. He promised. He's always doing that.'

I said, 'I'll talk to him. It might not make any difference, so don't build your hopes up, but I will talk to him. Promise me you won't do anything like that again, Elly? You didn't take anything else?'

'No,' she said. 'Mum, who was that man in our bathroom? Is he your boyfriend?'

I explained. 'Mum,' she said, 'I phoned Dad but he

181

was in a meeting, and then I phoned Nikki and I was on for quite a long time. I'll pay for it out of my Christmas money, I promise. It was just a cry frelp.'

I said, 'That's all right. You don't have to pay to try and talk to your daddy once in a while.'

'Mum,' she said, 'love you.'

'Love you too,' I said. 'You can pay for the pills if it'll make you feel better.' But she was asleep, tanked up on Hooper's Hooch and all those extra trace elements.

I went to Texas Homecare and spent my Road-Show expenses on paint and new lampshades and the biggest potted palm they'd got. I'm in the mood for a whole new look. White walls, stripped floors, jewel-bright cushions and cheap ethnic throws. We had this item on the programme yesterday, Fabulous Interiors on a Shoestring Budget, and like P. T. Barnum used to say, there's one born every minute.

I started stripping wallpaper, but I got an ache in my neck, so I thought I'd tackle the carpet instead. I wished I hadn't. There were some little white wriggly things underneath it and the floorboards don't look too good. And now I'm not even sure I want white walls. I'm starting to think womb-like crimson. Anyway, I reached the point of no return with a mountain of carpet blocking the doorway, and four different grades of sandpaper in the house, but nothing for dinner.

I asked Eleanor if she'd fetch something but she said

she was going roller-skating, could she have ten pounds, oh, and Uncle Philip phoned, this morning, or maybe it was yesterday.

I made a list:

Price single fare to Boston.

Ditto services of professional decorator.

Bergamot oil?

Give Galsworthy novels to Oxfam.

Cremate carpet.

Watercress with kumquats?

Whatever you are, be it.

Philip said, 'We've got a bit of a problem. Yvonne's back on G6 because she's had a bit of a set-back, and Mum's in the infirmary with blackouts. So the thing is, we shall have to split the visiting.'

I'd do anything: visit G6 every day, cook meat and potatoes for the little troglodytes, keep Yvonne's cleaning cloths properly segregated, anything sooner than sit by my mother's bed and experience time standing still.

I paid Yvonne a flying visit, just to give her a pile of magazines and tell her what I thought of her timing. She wasn't on G6 though, they'd moved her on to D3.

She said, 'I didn't plan it, I can tell you. Blummin' nuisance. This'll be twice I've had to cancel the time-share people.'

I asked her if there was anything she needed.

'Fresh set of insides,' she said. 'No, everything's

organized, thanks. I went to Freezacenters and did a big shop when the doctor told me I'd have to come back in here. Kayleigh's in charge of the washing this time, and Little Maureen's keeping an eye on Scott after school. You could remind Phil it's my week for turning the mattresses. And if you think of it, tape *Brookside* for me. I hate it when I get behind.'

I wandered across the landing to D2 on my way out. I had this crazy idea I might bump into that nice man who liked my marmalade ice-cream. The nurse on the desk didn't know anything about a Mrs Sullivan, but a big black cleaner, bursting out of her overall, said she thought she remembered her and she'd probably gone home.

I don't think there's anything wrong with my mother. She just wanted a bottle of Lucozade and a bit of fuss, and the doctors' rounds; she loves that. Telling the whole rigmarole over and over to the students, about feeling faint in Pricerite and steadying herself against the muesli shelf till somebody noticed and sent for a first aider, doing all the voices and actions, winking and simpering at everything the consultant says. It's funny because she never really went in for men. When she was younger, and not a bad-looking woman, you never saw her flirt with anyone, like the bread man or Uncle Dennis next door, or the paraffin delivery man.

Everything used to be delivered then. Milk, bread, potatoes, limeade and Dandelion & Burdock. Monday and Thursday was the butcher's van, Tuesday was the egg man from Dunton Bassett with a cleft palate, Wednesday was Roy's Mobile Greengrocery, and Friday was the chipper and the man from the Pru for the insurance money. Men were beating a track up and down that path all day long, but she was always ready for them with her big brown purse and the right money, to prevent them hanging about, counting out change and getting too chummy. *Travelling Fish Fryer Seduces Mother of Two.* I never saw her making up to any of them, but she does it now, in that quilted bedjacket, schmoozing up to the main man, occupying a bed and wasting my time when I should be in Birmingham. Her face dropped when she saw me. She said, 'I thought it'd be Philip. Where's Philip?'

I said, 'Philip's needed at home, Mum. Yvonne's back in hospital. She needs him there.'

She said, 'He'll come another time. There'll be other times. Mr Fitzgerald's putting me on the waiting list for a new hip.'

I told her the latest on Yvonne, but she was rummaging in her locker, looking for barley sugars. She said, 'Carry on, I am listening.' Why do people do that? It's not just her. I know hundreds of people who do it, looking away, fiddling in their handbag, searching for an ashtray and then saying, 'Yeah, carry on,' chopping what you're saying into little slices so that your point gets completely lost. I'd like to do the same thing to them, only I can't. I listen attentively, whatever their drivel, and they go away thinking they've had me rapt with fascination. Aunty Phyllis listened. I must get it from her.

Mum said, 'Well, I think her trouble's those diet drinks. I've always said so. They don't suit everybody. And there was no need for her to diet anyway. She's always been as thin as a lath, not like you. Mr Fitzgerald says my bones are turning to powder.'

I said I thought we should let the doctors decide about Yvonne. I said they don't usually do operations for blockages and give people tablets that make them feel sick, without some very good reason, but I was forgetting that my mother has never missed an episode of *Cardiac Arrest*.

'Well,' she said, 'the doctors don't always know. They told Mrs Sanderson's Harry he'd got acid indigestion and then his heart gave out in Marshall and Snelgrove's. They said your dad shouldn't keep syringeing his ears, but they didn't have to live with him. They didn't know how deaf he could be. Has Philip told them about the diet drinks? She shouldn't have to keep going away all the time, a woman with a family. She should be at home with those kiddies. I should have had my prolapse done in 1958, but you have to soldier on when you've got kiddies. I've told Philip, I've sent him a floral notelet, and I've told him you'll give him some money to get her a bottle of tonic wine, from me. How much would it be, do you think? Would two pounds do it?' And she started rummaging in her locker again for money.

I said, 'Mum, leave it. I'll get her the wine and tell her you sent it. It doesn't matter about the money. Just stop writing, telling Philip everything he's doing wrong. Do you think she'd be there a minute longer than she had to be? You know what she's like. She has to have more tests.

She could hardly hold a cup when I saw her at the weekend.'

'Tests!' she said. 'That's another thing. They do more harm than good. Your Uncle Cyril was never the same after he'd had tests. Sometimes you've just got to buck up and get on with it. Sometimes it's a question of mind over matter and a lot of top doctors agree with that. I was reading about it in *Reader's Digest*. The mind is a very powerful thing. Now guess who that is in the bed opposite? The chubby woman with the tight perm? You won't recognize her, I didn't, but she knew me; she said I never change. Remember the Glover girl? Didn't you used to play with her once upon a time? She was in your class at Lansdowne Road, and there was a sister, a bit older than Philip? Well, that's the mother. She's seen you doing your cooking. Go over and say hello to her.'

I did. Anything for a break from the medical wisdom of Muriel Clarke.

I said, 'Mrs Glover? Do you really remember me?'

'Course I do,' she said. 'We watch you on the telly. Never miss you. I was telling your mum, I had my bunions done. Did she tell you? Had them done, went home and then swelled up like a balloon with a blood clot, so here I am again. Bed rest. It gets on your pippin.'

She said Gillian had had her problems. Got pregnant and had a little boy, but they never knew who the father was, and Gillian couldn't really manage on her own. 'We had Glenn,' she said, 'from when he was three, so we've

189

had our hands full. You think you're finished with high-chairs and all that, and then things happen. You never know. Course, he's grown up now. He's in the army, in the catering corps, and he's got a young lady in Aldershot so . . . Makes you feel old. Anyway, Gillian's better than she was. She was on tranquillizers for a long time, but she's got a little maisonette now, just round the corner from us, and she's seeing somebody, so things are looking up for her. And Susan's got two girls, but they're down in Essex so we don't see as much of them as we'd like. You wouldn't remember Susan. Oh, here he is. He's had his head stuck in a book again and forgot the time. I'd given you up, Ron Glover.'

I asked her to remember me to Gillian. Like anyone would want to be remembered to that little thug. *Valium Mum Ate My Mintoes: Celebrity Relives Playground Terror.*

Kim's back, with $200 highlights, and presenting the show solo because Stuart is still on holiday. Tiff says Kim must have shed 10lb at least, but I don't know. She sounds so full of Californian shite I'd have thought she must be heavier.

She said, 'Left brain enhancement. You should try it sometime. You see, my audience needs me to be assertive and decisive. They know this is a live show and they put themselves in my hands, like I'm their pilot. When they can see I'm in command it makes them feel safe to relax and enjoy. You need balls to accept that kind of responsibility and I've got them.'

I was doing pancakes, between some flamenco dancers from Harpenden and the child with the peanut allergy who was almost killed by her grandma's kiss. Louie was on early between Knitting Clinic and How to Achieve the Sense and Sensibility Look with a Hotbrush. He said, 'This show gets worse. What about us men? What about all those redundant steelworkers sitting at home while the little woman's out learning computer skills? We should have things for them too. Clutch replacement without tears. Stronger forearms in two weeks. Anyway, listen . . . Chas has proposed. I wasn't going to tell you yet, but now I've blurted it out. He's looking at a place in Cornwall and he wants me to clean up my act and become his long-time companion. And he's got this contact in Cape Town who's looking for a monthly star-signs columnist to syndicate in southern Africa and it's as good as mine if I say the word. I could become a household name in Zimbabwe. I'm not sure how I'd fill the other twenty-eight days of the month, but I could try it I suppose. I could disappear from the astrology scene here and then rise from the ashes. I could present a game show or write a novel. And if it doesn't work out with Chas I can always go to Morocco and die of excess. What do you think, heart? Are you seeing Uncle Meredith later? I am.'

Tiff's enormous already. They don't wear maternity tents any more. She's still in her little Lycra dresses, pulled so tight you can see where her belly button's turned inside out. I asked her what the word was on Stuart and she said, 'Well, officially he's coming back, but my Neil's heard he's up for a sports programme on Sky, and the other thing is, Cliff Lassiter was back in yesterday. Meredith had him and Kim out to lunch.'

I said, 'But the Lassiters are a twin-pack. If Cliff comes Janey comes and if Janey comes, Kim's out.'

'No, no,' she said, scratching her stretch marks and waving her mascara wand, 'you mean you haven't heard about the widely rumoured Lassiter rift? Where have you been? Well, Janey's favourite for a big new travel show, but on her own, and the driver they had when they were standing in for Kim and Stuart, he reckoned they never spoke, all the way in from Kidderminster and all the way back. So I think Cliff'll come here and do the show with Kim. I hope he does, Cliff's nice. What do you think of the name Brook for a girl? Or Jordan? Neil says I'm wasting my time thinking about it because he knows it's going to be a boy, and it's going to be called Garth. I think Darcy's nice for a boy though. Isn't Kim looking great? She had one of those colonic thingydoodahs, you know? Flushed out all her toxins. And now she's doing the food-combining diet. Like, you can have bread, or you can have cheese, but you can't have bread and cheese. And you can have meat and carrots, but you can't have meat and potatoes. Or something like that. All the big stars do it.'

Louie came looking for me after he'd seen Meredith, but I was with one of the flamenco dancers, trying out her shoes, so he just did his Queen Mum wave and shot through.

I said, 'I saw it once in Torremolinos and I've always fancied having a go.'

'Go for it,' she said. 'I only tried it for a laugh at the leisure centre open day, but then I signed up. Made myself a skirt. Did my legs with Fast Tan. It's like the blues. It's like dancing the blues. My husband says it's been like having a new woman.'

I tried it all on then: shawl, earrings, carnation in my hair. Tiff said, 'Suits you. It's true then? About Louie?'

And that was when I found out he'd been sacked, effective forthwith, because the show's getting a whole new look, including Perry Peters, astrologer to royalty.

I said, 'It's because of the court case. I knew they'd get him for it.'

But Tiff said, 'No, it's not. The ratings went up after he'd been in the papers. It's because Meredith found out he doesn't really draw the charts. Meredith found out he just copies the ones in the magazines and puts a few extra bits in, so he had him in and called him an effing charlatan, but if anybody asks, we're to say he's leaving to pursue other interests and he'll be greatly missed. I don't believe he did make it all up. He said I'd be moving house and I did. He said Kim'd be going on a journey and she did. And he was nice too. Alison says he was all white and shaking. She says he just went; he never even dropped in to the canteen to say goodbye.'

I tried phoning the flat but it was too soon, and then all the way home I kept trying him on my mobile, but he wasn't there. I couldn't go round. I'd promised Philip I'd take hand cream and the new Jilly Cooper in for Yvonne.

I've been inside hospitals more in the past few months

than in my whole life before. Today felt different though. The smell, and people's shoes squeaking on the Vinolay, and the regulars who've had every operation in the book and know all the tea-bar volunteers by name; it all put me in a panic. I wanted to spring Yvonne out of there before it gobbled her up. But she was all right. She said, 'They're packing me off home again on Friday; they're fed up with me. I watched you do pancakes this morning. I told everyone you were my Phil's sister, so we had you on the telly in the day-room. I thought you looked really nice in that blue.'

The deal is, she's allowed home but she's on bed rest and liquid meals and there'll be a district nurse calling in most days till her stitches come out. Philip's supposed to be taking a week off from work, but she said, 'That's what he thinks. I shan't want him underfoot, getting goo all over the bottom of the iron. I can manage with Maureen. I tell you what you could do though. Scott's got to do something for school – a project. I can't remember what he's got to do, but if you could sort him out that'd be a help. I told him "Ask your Aunty Lizzie; she's the one's got all them books."'

I told her about Louie.

She said, 'Never. It won't happen, you'll see. They won't let him go. People'll write in and they'll have to keep him on; Rita will. And what's happening with this Bernard? Are you going to bring him round so we can have a look at him or what?'

195

I tried Louie again from the pay phone outside D2, but there was no reply. I was just setting off down the stairs when I saw Tom Sullivan, and I went right up to him, bounding up like he was an old friend.

I said, 'I did ask after you, when I was visiting before, but they said they thought Mrs Sullivan had gone home.'

'No,' he said, 'she died. I'm just back with some chocolates for the nurses. Well, how grand to see you. I've been intending to write to you at the programme. It's such a treat to see someone still cooking with butter sometimes, and making lovely puddings. I just wanted you to know. Are you visiting your friend still? Your sister?'

I waited while he took his chocolates to the nurses' station and then we walked down together. He said, 'That's me finished here. I'm relieved to see the back of this place. They were very good to Barbara, and they knew how things stood at home. They kept her here until just before the end; their timing was perfect. She was home for two days, quite comfy and peaceful, and then she went in her sleep. It couldn't have happened better; it's just the rest of it I've got to get through now. The boys have taken it hard. They keep saying there must have been something more that could have been done for her, but there really wasn't. And the neighbours. Half of them cross the street when they see me coming and the other half are in and out all the time with plates of dinner, like I'm a cat they've been asked to feed.'

We got to my car and I said, 'My sister-in-law's going

home on Friday.' And then he asked me if I'd have afternoon tea with him at the Astoria Court one day soon. He said, 'The scones are like brickends, but they do a very nice cherry Genoa and there's a little dance band plays on Fridays and Saturdays.'

I guess this means I've got a date. Saturday at three, I've got a date with a nice normal man who thinks I'm a famous and brilliant TV cook. Be still my fluttering heart.

Eleanor was on the phone to Alec again when I got home. I hope he realizes what moving to Boston is going to cost him. The good and amazing news was, she'd been tidying up. Dishes and cups I haven't seen in weeks, washed and sparkling on the draining-board and spoons from long-forgotten yoghurts. And then, when I went in to ask her not to be long on the phone, more surprises; she'd tied her hair back in a beautiful herring-bone plait, and the unravelling monster cardigan was nowhere to be seen, just a nice clean shirt and a bright smiley face. She said, 'Hi, Mum. Nikki's definitely having twins.'

It was late before I got any answer at Louie's. Chas picked up, but he wouldn't let me speak to Louie. He said, 'He's in no mood. He really thought he could trust you, of all people. I thought so too.'

I protested a bit, swore I didn't know what he was talking about, but I sort of did. It was dawning on me, slowly and horribly, that I'd done something, said something I shouldn't have. That whatever people really thought about his horoscopes we were all meant to go along with it, with a nudge and a wink maybe, but never saying anything to blow the gaff. I said, 'Meredith always knew; he must have done. And it doesn't matter. Louie always said it didn't matter that he was a fake because they're all fakes. He always said the main thing was to be a really great fake.'

Chas said, 'It matters when a woman like Kim starts saying things. What on earth were you doing even talking to her? I didn't think you had anything to do with her. Do you have any idea how much damage a woman like that can do? She's ousted Stuart and now Louie. I'd watch my back if I were you. If they'll drop Louie, they'll do anything.'

I begged Chas to let me speak to him, but he said he was asleep and they were leaving first thing, taking a holiday to recover and make plans. He said, 'Knowing Louie he'll forgive you. Just give him time. He'll call you when he's ready. He knows where to find you.'

I lay awake for hours. All the nice things that had happened, like bumping into Tom, and Elly moving her *Just Seventeen* magazines off the stairs, and Alec getting himself hamstrung with twins who'll be doing resits and ruining his gearbox when he really ought to be retired and playing a bit of golf and going on cruises, everything tasted sour because all I could think about was

199

Louie. I got up at four, had a whisky and wrote him a letter, only he won't get it for weeks. Weeks and weeks of Louie not being my friend. Then I made a banana sandwich and wrote a list:

Take up flamenco.
Plot Kim's downfall.
Scott.
Buy something elegant for the Astoria.
Spend more time with Eleanor.
Potatoes with anchovies and cheese? Or cream?

Eleanor was up and out early, so it looks like she really has turned over a new leaf. Just as well I didn't make any rash promises last night though, about leather jackets or holidays in the sun, because the bank wrote to tell me Alec's cheque bounced again and I'm more overdrawn than they would wish to see. So cleaning up my violet two-piece is about as elegant as I'm going to manage for afternoon tea with Tom.

I phoned my mother, but only after I'd found about fifty other little jobs to do first: scrubbing grease off the knurled knobs on the front of the cooker, rubbing finger-marks off the wall around all the light switches, sharpening all my pencils.

'Well, let's hope that's that,' she said, when I told her Yvonne was being allowed home. 'I was beginning to think she might have one of these syndromes. Mrs Sanderson's granddaughter's gone down with a syndrome, and she's been back and forth seeing specialists and they still can't fathom it.'

Anyway, the social services have promised to get her measured for a handrail by the bath, the couple at number twenty-seven that she never liked because they've had a car with no wheels in their front garden dragging the neighbourhood down, they're being repossessed by the building society, and Jack Lemmon's announced he's got no plans to retire. So, a pretty high feel-good factor in Glenville Close today.

Tea was great, even though my jacket smelled a bit of Dabitoff and the skirt seems to have shrunk. We had cucumber sandwiches and tomato, and fruit cake and coffee éclairs, and then Tom wheeled me round the little dance floor. I told him I didn't know any proper dances, but he said that was no impediment and it was dead easy doing tiny steps to 'I'll be Seeing You' and discovering we're both in favour of the removal of tomato skins. He said, 'Barbara always left them on, but I always take them off. Then what I like to do is cut the tomatoes in half and tuck a tiny sliver of garlic down inside each segment. Then I brush them with oil and bake them till they're just slightly charred and I can't stand the waiting any longer, so I have to eat them with some crusty bread.'

I already thought he was lovely, with his kind eyes and his waist hanging over his trousers, but it was the tomatoes that really swung it. I put my cheek against his and scraped against a bit he'd missed when he shaved, and we danced the whole of 'These Foolish Things' without either of us saying a word.

Still no sign of Eleanor when I got in. I was glad. I knew I'd got a stupid grin on my face and, anyway, I just wanted to give the paprika chicken livers a final run-through and then soak my battered feet. I was in my robe, painting my toenails, when the phone rang. It was Alec.

He said, 'Are you out of your fucking fucking mind? You are just so fucking irresponsible. Don't you think I've got enough on my plate? I mean, do you have the faintest fucking idea? And a one-way ticket? One-way costs nearly as much as a return. Is it some kind of sick joke? You know, I've explained to you how I'm placed just now. I wrote and told Elly as well. And now this. You are off your fucking rocker. I've thought so for years. I've got Nikki here, supposed to be taking things easy. I've got meetings in Baltimore and Cleveland next week. I just cannot believe this. I'm putting Eleanor on.'

She said, 'Sorry, Mum. I just really wanted to see Dad.

He's mad at me, but Nikki doesn't mind; she said it'll be company. She said Dad'll calm down later.'

She'd done it. My girl. My Eleanor, who couldn't even get her 'Meet Keanu Reeves' competition entry form posted on time. She'd taken my Visa card, bought a ticket, got out of bed before lunchtime and onto the airport coach, caught a plane, all on her own.

I said, 'How did you find your way? Anything could have happened. You could have disappeared and we wouldn't have known where to start looking. What did you do when you got to Boston?'

She said, 'I got the Blue Line until it didn't go any further and then I asked a guy and he said a taxi'd be about twenty bucks out to Dad's place, so I phoned Nikki and she fetched me. It's really nice here. They've got forty channels on the telly. Mum? Will you be OK on your own?'

I said, 'I'd better talk to Alec again,' but she said he was having another Scotch and shouting at Nikki, so I promised to call tomorrow and then I went across to her room and lay on her empty bed, just to prove to myself that she really really had done it.

Scott's got to draw a plan of the inside of an Egyptian pyramid, write about how they were built, and take some things into school, things that might have been put in a burial chamber, like food and drink.

I picked him up after school today and took him to the central lending library. He seemed to shrink as we walked in there. I got him a junior ticket, I thought he'd like that, but really I think he'd sooner have had his teeth drilled. But then we looked at some books, with pictures of mummies with their bandages taken off, and he got very excited and kept saying 'wicked'. I read him a bit about the brain being drawn down through the nose by a hook, and the organs being taken out and preserved in separate little jars. We borrowed one of the books, so he could copy some hieroglyphics onto the front of his project, and a book about Aston Villa, and he was puffed back up to his usual size by the time we were ready to leave.

'Yeah,' he said, 'my mum brings me here all the time. I'm allowed twenty books, thirty books.'

I said, 'What kind of things do you think they had to eat, these Egyptians?'

'Beans?' he said.

I said, 'They might have. What else?'

'Chips?'

I said, 'I don't think so. I don't think they had potatoes in those days. You'll have to read your book and see if it says. What else?'

'Pop tarts?'

We were on our way down Corporation Street to get him a lined pad and some felt-tipped pens when I heard someone calling my name, and there was Tom, on his way to catch his train to London and spend a few days with his son.

He said, 'Well fancy that. Just when I was feeling sorry for myself, wishing I could see a nice friendly face, and there it is. Hello, young man.'

I said, 'We're doing the Egyptians. Show Tom the book we got, Scott.'

And he looked at us both like I'd addressed him in Swahili, dug his hands deep into his anorak pockets, and hoicked a great big sixty-Park-Drive-a-day gobbet of phlegm plumb onto the toe of Tom's suede shoes.

I fumbled around with Kleenex, with a red haze in front of my eyes, and Tom said, 'Never mind, don't worry, I'd best be off before I miss my train,' and disappeared into the crowd. Then the ants started up. They hadn't been around for a day or two, but they were back with a vengeance. So I hit Scott; I clouted him round the ear in a completely unpremeditated way, and then I did it again, with malice aforethought. It was still red when we got back to Yvonne and Philip's, but no one seemed to notice, and Scott kept quiet. Very quiet.

Today was my first show since Louie got the sack. I gave Kim the cold shoulder, but I don't know that she noticed because she was busying herself with the studio guests. Three vengeful ex-wives, and a senior citizen from Rednal, in for a make-over for her wedding to her long-lost wartime sweetheart.

It was nearly time for me to go on. I heard Kim say, 'For those of you who think a warm salad sounds a bit of a contradiction, let me tell you, when I was in California recently I ate nothing else, and you can see how much good they did me. We've got some fabulous warm-salad ideas coming up soon, but before that, the chanting monks who are this week's surprise chart-toppers. Experts say Gregorian chant is a great thing to listen to if you're getting stressed, sitting in a traffic jam, or if you can't sleep. I'll be getting the facts from our own Dr Mark, and I'll also be chatting to the monk who gave up chanting and took up *enchanting*, Il

Stregone, the Benedictine turned stage hypnotist. All this, right after the break.'

That was when I noticed Sandie Mulholland, pressing Meredith to her zebra-skin bosom. Since when does she turn up here, in the middle of a show she's not even appearing in, and since when does Hegarty think he can send any of his circus freaks onto my patch without at least letting me know?

I phoned him the minute I got home. I said, 'Hegarty, do you represent me or what?'

He said, 'What?'

I said, 'A and 1, you never call me, you never get me anything new, and you haven't even talked to me yet about next year's contract. B and 2, why was Sandie Mulholland sniffing round my show today, round my producer, in her wacky Zulu earrings and her wacky tie-dye turban?'

He said, 'Sandie knows Meredith, Meredith knows Sandie. It's called networking. And I have got something for you. There's a new cookery slot coming up in the autumn on *Kid's Stuff*. It's on now, Wednesdays at four, but no cookery. Take a look at it and let me know what you think. And let's talk, not now, now's not good. I've got the electrician here with bare wires and Jen's off with an abscess. But let's talk; let's talk real soon.'

I haven't heard from Tom and I'm not surprised. If I never see him again I'll be really sad, but at least I shan't have to die of shame all over again. I wish I could turn the clock back and make Yvonne not ill so I didn't have to get involved with her stupid ugly kids, and just have met Tom some other way and be having dinner with him. I'd have cooked a rack of lamb with a mustard and green herb crust, and an orange tart with chocolate pastry, and we'd probably listen to a Brandenburg concerto or two, and he might tell me some more about his wife, and I'd listen in a perfectly calm and comfortable way because you can't feel awkward about a dead person, even though her clothes may still be hanging in a cupboard upstairs.

Two messages when I got in: Eleanor to say, 'Dad says I might as well stay for a while so Nikki's not on her own so much. Can you post me my denim jacket?' and Philip to say, 'Yvonne says can you get some plug-in air fresheners, forest-pine flavour and bring them when you come? She says you'll know what to get.'

I wish Louie'd call as well.

There was a burst water main. They were digging up the road outside, a man with a pneumatic drill and two others watching him. I said, 'There's somebody trying to sleep in this house.' But they couldn't hear me.

Yvonne wasn't trying to sleep though. She was sitting up, doing a word puzzle in *Take a Break*, looking better than I'd seen her in weeks. Scott was at football, and Kayleigh had gone to Alton Towers with the youth club. Philip said, 'She fancies poached egg on toast. Is that the same as fried?' So I sent him to pick some daffodils to put on her tray while I poached two eggs and cut the crusts off her toast. I called up to ask her what she wanted to drink but she couldn't hear me for the drilling outside. I made tea, enough for the three of us.

He came in with hyacinths, pulled clean out of the ground. Yvonne's right, he never knows what to do unless you tell him exactly. Except if it's to do with cars or electrics. I said, 'She seems better this morning.'

He said, 'She is. She had a bad night, tossing and turning, but I think she's turned the corner. She's talking about hiring a carpet shampooer next weekend.'

I picked a few flower-heads off the stalks and put them on the tray. Then we carried it upstairs and watched Yvonne eat like we were watching our favourite animal at the zoo. The sun broke through, brilliant after the rain, and she said, 'Just look at the state of those windows. I'm going to give this place such a bottoming once I'm out of this bed.' The phone rang and I ran down to answer it. I heard Yvonne say, 'I hope you've not let us run low on Windolene. Why don't you clear off for half an hour? Put the car through the auto-wash? Lizzie'll sit with me.'

The girl said, 'This is Debbie calling, from Nationwide Easiglaze. We are presently in your area demonstrating our range of PVC and aluminium windows, doors and conservatories, and offering free no-obligation quotations. Would you be interested at all?'

Imagine that? Phoning up total strangers on a Saturday morning and reciting that little speech. And sometimes people say yes. Imagine that. There must be people sitting around thinking, 'Well, I'd buy a conservatory if only somebody'd phone me up and ask me.'

Then Philip called me from upstairs. He said, 'Can you bring some paper towels? The eggs haven't stayed down.'

Not just the eggs, a few pints of her blood too, by the look of his shirt and the duvet and the wallpaper opposite the foot of the bed. He was dabbing at it, saying she'd go spare if the duvet was ruined, and the drilling stopped, because it was time for the workmen to have a brew and read the racing page. There wasn't a sound, and the yolk was still wet on the plate.

I didn't know who to phone. I asked Philip if it should be for an ambulance or their doctor, but he just kept mopping, mopping. I phoned for both. The emergency switchboard asked me what was the problem and I didn't know quite what to say. I don't think you're supposed to say someone's dead; you're supposed to wait for an expert to say that. But I did say it, and they made me say the address twice and who I was, and my voice sounded a million trillion miles away.

When you die, your house fills up with people. They search for your tea caddy and fetch your washing off the line, and they speak very quietly. After they've seen you being taken away they don't say anything much at all for a while. The doctor sent the ambulance away and then, after a while, two men came in an unmarked van and went upstairs. Little Maureen went up with them and Big Rita tidied up the kitchen, so it was a fitting monument to Yvonne, although there wasn't really anything to tidy, and then we just sat. We could hear them moving about over our heads. 'Last offices,' Rita said, and Philip said, 'What do you think happens next?'

When we were kids there was a woman who was sent for when people died at home. Her name was Mrs Hammond and she did dress alterations as well and iced cakes. You always knew when she'd got a call-out because Mr Shakespeare the undertaker'd drive round in his black

Rover and knock on her door, and it was something of an event. *Big Car In Glenville: Third Sighting This Year.*

When it was going to be our nana and grandad's golden wedding someone said to Mum, 'Are you having Mrs Hammond do the cake?' but she said she wouldn't fancy it, in case she'd been out on some other business and forgotten to wash her hands. I told Philip once that Mrs Hammond came round when she saw a magpie on your roof because that meant somebody was going to die really soon and she brought her tape measure to size you up for a shroud. I told him because I knew she was coming round to see if she could let down the hem of his school mac, and when he saw her at the door with her tape measure he hid behind the settee and cried. Then I threatened him with a Chinese burn to ask Mum exactly what Mrs Hammond did to dead people, but she gave him a whack for pestering her, so he got it on both arms that day.

Mum iced the cake for the golden wedding, only she gauged it wrong and she had to squash on congratulations And Grandad died before the party, of worry probably about the expense, so Mrs Hammond got in on the act anyway and did her secret things.

There aren't any Mrs Hammonds now. You're not supposed to die at home any more and leave a stain on the mattress. I knew they were just tidying her up before they carried her out. Yvonne would have liked the idea of being tidied up.

Little Maureen came down. She said, 'They're ready to go now.' I ran outside to make sure the men from the water board weren't hanging about, or anyone just coming by with their Tesco bags, but the street was empty. I never saw a Saturday street so empty. And she was out, into the van and gone. To the Co-op chapel of rest.

I said to them, 'She looked better.' But Rita shook her head.

She said, 'When I saw the colour of her yesterday and she started talking about doing the carpets, I thought "Aye, aye. I don't like the sound of this."'

Maureen said, 'I'll fetch Scott from football. I'll keep him till his daddy's ready. And Rita'll have Kayleigh, only she's not due back till nine. You go in to Phil. There'll be people need telling.'

It was too early to call Boston. I called her brother in Walsall. He said, 'Oh dear, oh dear. When do you think they'll have the funeral? We're flying to Tenerife next Friday.'

Mum said, 'Oh no. Say it isn't true. How can it be? Tell me that. How can he have taken her and left a useless old woman like me? I didn't know things were that bad. Did you know things were that bad? Should I come? You'll have to fetch me, I can't manage those big steps up to the coach. Why ever did you want to go feeding her eggs. Everybody knows how eggs lie. A drop of warm milk would have been better. Oh what a terrible shock. I shall just have to have a quiet sit down. Take it in. You

216

can't hardly take it in, can you? I'm glad you're there with him. That's something, at any rate.'

Philip was watching *Football Focus*, still in the same shirt. I said I'd soak it, and he went back to the telly, sitting in his vest. He didn't cry till Scott came in after Maureen had given him his tea. Scott got him in an arm lock on the settee and said, 'It's all right, Dad. I'm going to look after you and everything.'

They both cried till they fell asleep. I threw a cover over them and sat in the dusk to wait for Kayleigh.

There was an envelope on the mat when I got home. I tried to open it one-handed while I called Boston.

Nikki said, 'Eleanor's out with Alec. They've gone roller-blading. She's no trouble to have here, you know? As long as you don't mind.'

I asked her about the babies before I told her my reason for calling.

'Oh,' she said, 'that's the most terrible thing. It's not fair, is it? How can that be fair when there are murderers and rapists who live to be ninety. And her children. Those poor children. And you're all on your own there. Do you want Elly to come home?'

There didn't seem any point.

She said, 'If it's the money, we'll find it. I know Alec's not been sending you anything, but he will do, as soon as we've got ourselves straight. We thought I'd be working, you see. We hadn't really planned on this happening.'

I was hardly listening to her in the end. She'd destroyed

218

my bimbo-usurper fantasy. She was supposed to be a gold-digging vixen, leeching Eleanor's birthright and spending it on corkscrew perms, and then tragically losing her sanity and her looks, haunted by the spectre of her beautiful and still powerful predecessor, i.e. me. But now it turns out she's just some soft-hearted kitten, lumbered with Alec and his three children and his cash-flow crises and his endless meetings somewhere too far to get home for the night. Anyway, I'd managed to get the gist of my letter between murmuring things to Nikki and my heart was trying to bang its way out of my chest. . . . *decision taken . . . In the Kitchen will not continue in its present form . . . new contract will not therefore . . . like to take this opportunity . . .*

They sacked me. Just like that. And my picture's on the front of their recipe book. This is Kim's doing. Chas was right. It's Kim's doing and Hegarty's. They've given my spot to Sandie Mulholland. They're going to work her up into a big-time celebrity because the cameras like her kaftans, but she knows shit about food. They're making a very big mistake.

I sat up all night dialling Tom's number even though I know he's at his son's and he won't ever want to see me again anyway, and Louie's number, even though he blames me for his downfall and his flat's all closed up and the blinds are drawn. I drank gallons of coffee and ate everything in the fridge except the Parmesan cheese, and

I tried to write down things I could do for money but I only got as far as:

Cash in premium bonds.

Prostitution.

and I kept wondering if Yvonne was all right in the chapel of rest, and if she knew. She couldn't have done. Even Yvonne wouldn't have been bothered about Windolene at a time like that. I hope she didn't know.

I spent the whole morning trying to buy something black in a size eighteen. I was in the wrong kind of shops. I thought I still bought things in boutiques where the sales-girls have got lovebites, but maybe that was last year. I had to get black ties too, for Philip and Scott, and Scotch and sherry, and ham for Maureen and Rita to make sand-wiches. Then I drove to the outsize store in Halesowen and got a long-line trouser suit with a Nehru collar and pearl buttons and a drape-collar blended cashmere coat because Yvonne always said I should wear pillar-box red. I'll talk to the bank when I'm good and ready.

The flowers started arriving soon after breakfast time and we put them along the foot of the garage door until the Co-op men came for them. Her brother was early too, and he made a start on the Scotch. He said his wife couldn't get the time off work.

Mum kept saying Scott and Kayleigh should have been sent away for the day, and Maureen said they were old enough to decide for themselves, and Yvonne's brother said it was the saddest day of his life. Philip disappeared. I left it a few minutes and then I went looking for him. He was in the outhouse next to the kitchen trying to remember which cloth he was supposed to use for condensation on windows. I gave him a big hug and he screwed his eyes up tight to get rid of the tears.

He said, 'I've asked for "Lord of the Dance". Do you think that'll be suitable? She did like that.'

The inside of my throat ached from being the big strong sister.

He said, 'And when the cars come, I want you and Mum in with me and Scott and Kayleigh. He reckons he should be in the first car because he's her brother, but he's never been nigh nor by all the while she's been poorly, and anyway, they had different dads.'

Still the flowers kept coming, from the Leccy Board, and people who'd known her in Walsall, and Alec and Nikki and Eleanor, fast asleep in Boston, Massachusetts.

Kayleigh held my hand when we got into the car and hid her face. Mum said, 'Scott, you come here and look out of this window with your nana, tell her what makes these cars are.' But he wouldn't. His eyes never left the hearse in front of us.

He said, 'My mum's not in that box.'

She said, 'Course she's not. She's in heaven with Grandad Wilf and Nana and Grandad Slater.'

He said, 'That's an empty box. My mum quickly jumped out of it and ran back to the hospital to get better.' And then he put his fingers in his ears, just like Philip did when I tried to tell him why Bugsie wasn't in his hutch any more.

I hadn't had anything all morning except aspirin. The crematorium chapel started revolving and I had beads of cold sweat on my top lip. I went outside and heaved onto a floral tribute from 'All at Kleeneezee Direct Sales'. Scott had followed me out there, watching. He said, 'My mum used to be sick sometimes, and now

223

she's going to be all burned up. You've got sick on your chin.'

The house was packed with people I didn't know, so I stayed in the kitchen with Rita and Kayleigh, making pots of tea as fast as the kettles would boil, and Scott didn't budge from my side. He said, 'Where's your girl?' and when I told him he said, 'We're going to America. Dad's taking us to Disney and we're going to hire a camper van.'

I could hear my mother expounding her diet-drinks theory to Yvonne's aunty from Tipton, and her brother getting quarrelsome, but Rita kept washing and I kept drying, and Yvonne kept grinning at us, watching the birdie, from the Hunkies' UK Tour souvenir photo on the fridge door.

My last show. Meredith made himself scarce. There was me thinking he was trying to get up the courage to ask me out and all the while he was trying to find a nice way to dump me. Kim was in make-up ahead of me explaining again to Tiff what a seminal experience it had been, balancing her brain in San Francisco.

She said, 'Most women find it hard to get in touch with their male side. You know? But I've done a lot of work on this. It isn't for everyone, Tiff. I wouldn't say it was for you.'

Tiff said, 'No, I wouldn't try anything that might harm the baby. And I don't think it sounds like the kind of thing Neil would let me do. He's a bit funny like that.'

Kim said, 'Well, there you are. I'm in a different position. I live alone, work alone, I've put myself through a lot of emotional pain on this one, Tiff, and now I am man, I am woman and I am island.'

Tiff said, 'Mm. It does sound fascinating. And was it an actual operation you had?'

I said, 'Yes. They bored a hole in her skull, sucked her brains out with an upholstery nozzle, and replaced them with the stuff from her colon.'

She yanked her make-up cape from round her shoulders and swept out. She said, 'Thank you, Tiffany, I'll do my own hair. At least Louie left with some dignity.'

The woman who ran off with her daughter's fiancé was on first, then Easy-To-Make Swags and Pelmets, Preparing for Spring in Your Greenhouse, and the Valerie Tobin Bikini Action Plan. I was so glad about the way the schedule had worked out. I'd have hated to finish on some low-calorie theme that made it look like victory for Tobin.

The smell of melted chocolate had everyone twitching, and then Kim got orders through her earpiece, to gather everyone round me to sample the chocolate and raisin refrigerator cake and do a big chummy wind-up. Kim, Tobin, the pelmet woman, and Stan who does gardening tips, all issued with plates and forks.

Kim said, 'Well, that's about it for this morning. Sadly we're saying goodbye to Lizzie Partridge today. She's getting out of the kitchen and moving on to new and exciting things I'm sure. Stan's tucking in already I see. How about you, Valerie? Do chocolate cakes shake your resolve?'

Tobin was smiling, glassy-eyed, with her cake untouched.

'Never,' she said. 'Once you've followed the Tobin Low-Fat Plan and achieved your lovely new shape you're really not tempted to break the rules ever again. And you know, Kim, people are wising up. They're learning that you don't need food like this, and if you want to look good and feel good you just kick it out of your life for good.'

I had no previous experience of smacking people in the mouth, but I think Tobin did. I swung with my left and clipped her nose enough to draw blood, and damn me if the miserable little bag of bones didn't swing straight back at me with her right and get me full in the mouth with her sapphire and diamond cluster. I felt my front teeth go. That did it. I've always had perfect teeth. I grabbed the back of her head and brought her down hard onto the mocha ginger pavlova, and then I ran with her, dragging her by her head and smashed her face right up against the lens of Camera One. We were off-air by the time Kim tried to pull me off her and the floor manager tried to pull Kim off me, but I know, because I found out later, that the last thing viewers saw was Tobin's face flattened against the glass with ganache and cream and meringue. Perfect meringue. I felt as strong as an ox. I bit Kim's hand till she let go, then I gave all three of them an eyeful of five-minute chocolate mousse and a good sharp knee in the abdominals for Tobin. It was all over in less than a minute.

There was meringue everywhere and two of my teeth

in there somewhere too. They fetched Geordie and Jim, their two biggest security gorillas, to escort me to the green room, and sent for a nurse for Tobin, and then the police came, and we could hear Meredith talking her out of making a complaint, and Kim saying, 'Don't give her the satisfaction,' and Alison screaming that the switchboard was swamped. Geordie winked at me and said, 'Another giant step for mankind, pet.'

They said I was free to go and that my agent was outside. But it wasn't Hegarty, it was Tom Sullivan, and he'd come in such a hurry he was wearing his slippers.

The phone hasn't stopped. I've had six requests from daytime chat shows, an invitation to speak at the Diet Smashers' conference in June, a completely disgusting suggestion from Amsterdam, and serious proposals from three Sunday papers. Then there were messages from Big Rita to say, 'Knockout. Philip's booked to go to Disney and the kids seem all right. Scott's bragging about you.' From Eleanor to say, 'Just heard. Awesome. Dad says I can stay. Can I?' And from Izzard Sykes who want to commission a book for their *Pleasures of the Table* series, and my mother who said she had hoped she'd brought me up to behave nicely.

It was good to get away from it all yesterday, once the dentist had finished patching me up. A brisk walk in the sea air and an icy paddle and a fried-fish supper on the Palace Pier with mushy peas and champagne.

I slept deep and late. It was ten o'clock when I went down to pick up the mail and grind some coffee. I knew that writing.

It said:

Well done, thou good and trusty friend. Jupiter's arrival at the mid-heaven of your chart heralds positive developments and an end to a period of disappointment and loss. You are on the threshold of a bright tomorrow, with a long journey in the offing, possibly without benefit of a buffet-car service due to operational difficulties. You'll have to change at Truro, get the Falmouth train, and I'll meet you at Penryn. Bring your wellies and the new Peter Ackroyd if it's out before you come. I've hated not being friends with you. I need you to visit. It's fucking paradise down here, heart. I need you to bring a little dark relief. And it's all right with Chas. He says if you bring your recipe book you can stay for ever. And Hershey chocolate syrup. How long would it take that ex of yours to mail you some cans of Hershey? The house is nice now we got rid of the tangerine curtains and the kitchen's got everything. You know Chas. It's even got a larding needle. Come soon. Bring a man if you've found a nice one. And don't let's ever talk about you know what. I've missed you, Lizzie Partridge. I've missed you *this* much. Yours, Louie.

229

I made coffee and took the letter back to bed. I said, 'What do you think?' and Tom reached for his reading glasses.